Dead on the Water

By
R.W.K. Clark

This is a work of fiction. All names, characters, locales, and incidents are
the product of the author's imagination. Any resemblance to actual
people, places, or events is coincidental or fictionalized.
Published in the United States by Clarkltd.
Po Box 45313 Rio Rancho, NM 87174
info@clarkltd.com

Revised 2020
Edition 1

United States Copyright Office
TX8-298-991 July 2016
1-8908249402 June 2020
1-9070547291 July 2020

Library of Congress Control Number: 2017907158
International Standard Book Numbers
ISBN-13: 978-0997876703 (Amazon)
ASIN: B01J85V8Y4 (Kindle)
ASIN: B075TF3Q7B (Audio)

/200907

CONTENTS

ACKNOWLEDGMENTS

I dedicate this novel to my wonderful readers and for all the amazing people I've met and those I haven't. To my family and loved ones, all your support will not be forgotten.

Special thanks to Robert Lawrence, and my fiancée Hope Safford for their encouragements.

This book was made possible by reviews from readers like you.

Thank you

PROLOGUE

"Bruce, grab the injections, let's get started." Anson was saying as he cleared his throat and began his dictation into the recorder. "This is Doctor Anson audio log Friday, December 31, 2019. Inducing serum 744 part A on test subject, the time is 1:30 pm."

Bruce watched as he rambled on into the recorder. "The male rat subject is showing all normal vital signs," Bruce stated in a professional tone.

"I will now restrict the air supply to the airtight container to induce suffocation." Anson was saying into the device.

Bruce acknowledged and proceeded to watch for loss of consciousness while turning over all the years he had worked under Anson. He had to admit it; he was comfortable, until recently. Having to uproot from the United States because of illegal animal testing made Bruce uneasy. He never imagined himself living in a third world country.

"Notate the time of death," Anson said, startling Bruce, snapping him out of his trance.

Bruce looked up at the clock and hastily jotted down the time of death, as Doctor Anson spoke into the recorder again.

"Neuronal activity has ceased, Doctor," Bruce stated as he notated the time.

"Open the air sealed containment unit, and I will initiate serum 744 part B," he commanded, with a determined yet hopeful tone to his voice.

Bruce watched as the Doctor proceeded to apply light rhythmic pressure to the treated subject."

"It's alive," Anson exclaimed in an overzealous tone. "The rat has returned. This is it; finally, I have done it after all these years. I have successfully found a way to bring the dead back to life. Do you realize what this means, Bruce? Endless funding, Nobel prize the list goes on my boy."

Bruce studied the rat as terror fell over him. "This rodent is not the same, Doctor. It's way too aggressive." Bruce stated in a matter of fact tone. With a horrified look on his face. He shouted, "the pest has transformed into a zombie."

Anson was in a dreamy trance calculating the fame he had desperately wanted. "This is perfect," Anson was saying as he stopped abruptly in mid-sentence. "What did you say?" Bruce's comment snapped the Doctor out of his reverie. "Zombie?" He exclaimed, "Are you crazy, Bruce? It's alive; I've discovered a miracle."

CHAPTER 1

Adam Harrington turned on his new video game unit, laying back on his bed, with his controller in hand. He was thinking about how he had been anticipating the release of this brand new game. He just knew it was going to be the best criminal role-playing game ever. It had not been released to the public yet, but his father had connections, so he got it before anyone else. His friends would just die when they found out. The thought made him feel smug, and Adam Harrington enjoyed feeling smug.

As he played, his head bobbed to the heavy metal song pumping from the surround sound speaker system in his room. He was smiling, and his heart was beating hard with joy. Just then, he could have sworn he heard a scream from down the hall. His fingers paused over the controller, and his head stopped bobbing as he listened. All was still, so he went back to his game. Probably just his big sister having a fit of some kind.

Suddenly his bedroom door flew open. His mother Claire stood in the doorway, her face flushed and tears on her cheeks as she panted at him, "Adam, come now! There is a massive spider in my shower, and I want it gone!"

"Mom," Adam replied with disgust, "Can't you see I'm busy?"

Hysterical Claire hollered, "I don't care if you are dying, Adam Harrington. Now!" She turned and stomped off down the hall, leaving his door wide open.

"Geez!" Adam yelled. "Why can't you do anything for yourself?" He threw the controller down on his bed and stood up, kicking one of his shoes out of the way for good measure. His mother was so annoying. He knew that parents were annoying to most twelve-year-olds, but it was always something with this woman. If it wasn't a spider making her scream, she was screaming because she couldn't find her credit card. Mother or not, she was a mess.

He went to her room to find her on the bed, feet up off the floor. "In the shower?" he asked, and she nodded at him, tears falling from her eyes.

"And make sure you clean it up after you kill it," she told him. "I'm certainly not going to touch that disgusting thing!"

Adam rolled his eyes and walked into the bathroom. "Of course not. I would never presume to make you do anything like this for yourself, madam." His sarcasm did not escape her, but she needed him to get rid of the spider, so she said nothing.

He walked into the bathroom and opened the glass door to the shower. There on the floor was a daddy-long-legs, and it was not even big. He shook his head in frustration and said under his breath, "Wouldn't want to dirty your manicured hands, now would we mother?"

Ariana could hear the commotion from down the hall. Did she really just hear her mother urge Adam to kill something? Right then, she made a b-line for her mother's room and barged in, causing Adam to stop in his tracks. He turned and looked towards the door. There stood Ariana, her eyes narrowed with a nit brow and asked Adam, "what do you think you're doing?"

"Our precious mother wants me to kill this spider," Adam stated rolling his eyes, yet again. "Don't you dare kill it, Adam!" she hollered.

In a flash, Ari snatched up the spider before Adam could grab it. "Adam, you dork," she said with contempt for his actions. "All life is sacred, and everything has a right to live fearlessly. Haven't you ever heard of Ahimsa?" She questioned as she coddled the poor innocent creature in her palm.

Adam rolled his eyes to Ariana's statement, and Claire was in utter shock that Ariana was touching the rancid pest with her hand. Claire quickly put her hand to her mouth in a failed attempt to keep herself from screaming. "Get that thing out of my room and the entire house for that matter, this instant young lady!" Claire shouted in terror. Ariana made her way out of the room. Now it was her turn to roll her eyes. This family will never understand the sanctity of life, she thought to herself.

Adam looked at his mother. "The job is done, your highness. You may resume your vital activities," he said to Claire with the same reluctance. Claire let out a massive breath and put her nose in the air. "Thank you, Adam. You don't have to be so brazen, you know. After all, I do everything for you."

"Whatever," he replied and returned to his room and his game.

With that horrible pest gone, Claire could concentrate.

When Ari was finally outside, she went straight for the bushes, "here you go, little fellow, there is plenty to eat out here." She said in a motherly tone as she turned the arachnid loose on a branch. Satisfied, Ariana returned to her room. Her quest was done.

The family was going to be enjoying a cruise to Belize, so Claire was sorting her clothes and packing. Her children should be doing the same, but she couldn't worry about that right now. She had to worry about herself.

She stood, checking the floor around her feet for spiders. With a shudder, she closed her eyes and shook her head as if to shake the reality of their existence from her mind. Horrid, nasty little things they were! But of course, she felt that way about any living thing that was smaller than a cat or a dog, and she didn't even really like those creatures either. Her daughter, on the other hand, was her complete opposite in that department. Claire would never understand Ariana's love for all things living.

The family would drive into Houston in the morning from their home in Royden Oaks, and from there, they would launch out to Belize. Oh, how she looked forward to the shopping, the dining and everything in between! She opened her massive closet and pressed the button, which made the hanger bars rotate. Dozens of outfits passed before her eyes, but after one rotation, she hit the stop button with disgust. She had absolutely nothing to wear! She supposed she would have to go shopping.

Claire went to her husband Jason's office, down the hall. She could hear his voice on the other side of the door. "No, Paul, I am not interested in that particular merger! There is nothing Intratech can offer us that we haven't already accomplished for ourselves, or won't in the future!" Claire opened the office door, just a crack, and poked her head inside. Jason looked up at her and gave her a gesture that said, "What the heck do you want?"

She stepped in and sat in the chair across from his desk to wait. "Listen, Paul. The family and I are leaving for our cruise in the morning. I need to be able to count on you to rid us of the burden of Intratech and their naggings. Can I do that? Count on you, I mean?" He said into the phone. Claire could hear Paul's incoherent rattling on the other end, then Jason said, "Good. I truly don't want to be bothered during my vacation. Prove to me that you can function without me holding your damn hand!"

Jason slammed down the receiver and looked at his wife. "What is it, Claire?" It was always something with her.

"I'm going to go shopping, and I wondered if there

was anything you needed for the trip," she said.

Jason raised his eyebrows. "What are you shopping for?"

"Well, I wanted to get some clothes, of course," she replied, then she looked down at her hands. "Or whatever."

He let out a ragged, exaggerated breath. "Are you kidding me?"

"I have nothing…" she began.

"You have everything!" Jason grumbled, his annoyance more than obvious. "Just go, and you may as well make sure the kids have what they want and need. Damn, you people are just going to be the death of me." He rose from his desk and went into the bathroom, closing the door behind him, mumbling about his miserable life under his breath. The conversation with Claire was over.

She stood and went to her daughter Ariana's room. Ariana had always had an obsession with becoming a veterinarian. Her first year of college had to be simply overwhelming, and Claire felt for the poor girl. Ariana would save every homeless, sick, and lonely animal in the world, if she could. Oh, the innocence of youth! She wanted so badly for her daughter to take an interest in the things she liked, such as shopping, but Ariana had her mind solidly set on a college degree. She would ask the girl to go shopping with her but doubted she would.

Claire tapped on her daughter's door. "Ari, do you want to go shopping with me?"

The door opened, and there stood her Ariana.

Behind her were clothes on her bed and an open suitcase; the girl was packing for the cruise. At least one of her children was somewhat responsible.

"For what?" Ariana questioned.

"Well," Claire replied, "Whatever you may want or need for the vacation."

"Mother, we all have everything we could possibly want or need," Ariana said.

Claire shrugged. "Well, I have nothing to wear…"

Ariana shook her head and rolled her eyes before shutting the door. After a year away at college, she did not miss her mom's antics. That was for sure. She had no desire to go shopping with the woman.

Claire put her nose in the air and shrugged off her daughter's obvious displeasure. Someday, the girl would understand.

More than likely, she would turn out just like her mother, and the thought pleased Claire's selfish ego to no end.

∞

Claire returned from shopping and was on the phone with the children with special needs support group, planning activities for Adam. "You know Claire; perhaps you should leave the videogames at home so you can bond with Adam," Janice was saying. "That always seemed to work with Andy. Taking away his source of distraction, always seems to pull him out of his shell. Forcing him to try new things." She continued.

"I agree with you he needs some interaction," Claire stated in a matter of fact tone. Claire thought quietly to herself; there is no way I'm leaving his videogames, while mentally rolling her eyes. That was the only way she could get a break from him. Truth be told Adam's entertainment was videogames, she used them for a distraction, otherwise dealing with his constant need for attention was more than she could handle.

Claire filled her wine glass to the top one more time. The sound of the bottle touching the glass and wine flowing was easily heard over the phone. "While I'm sure that works for you and Andy, that is not the case when it comes to Adam," Claire said with a snap to her voice. Why was it that every parent thought they knew what was best for her child? Adam wasn't like most kids, obviously, and she thought Janice would understand that. However, every time she got a chance to make Claire feel like a shitty parent, Janice was first to chime in.

"I know not all children are the same," Janice snapped back. "However, maybe if you focused more on Adam's needs and less on your wine, he may not have as many problems as he does."

Claire bit her lip to keep herself from yelling. She had enough, "Janice, I need to go before this conversation goes too far and ends our relationship; we're both extremely touchy when it comes to this subject. Besides, I need to pack. Have a great day."

Claire immediately hung up the phone. She topped her wine glass once again, as she walked to her room.

∞

Jason's afternoon appointment was going well. "I

hope this trip will bring us all closer together." He stated.

"Are you considering it to be a last attempt to save a troubled marriage?" His therapist Catherine asked.

Jason looked at Catherine, slightly nodding his head in agreement. "Yes, I suppose it is obvious I'm at the end of my rope, plus it's Ari's Birthday." Jason replied. "Ariana hasn't been around for the last year. It hasn't been easy, without my peacekeeper." Jason continued. "Since Ariana left for college, things have gotten progressively worse. She is back, so we're celebrating that too. I'm so proud of her; she is working on getting her degree in veterinary medicine."

"That is fantastic. How is Ariana handling the course load?" Catherine studied Jason's expression.

"She has my work ethic and all the brains in the family, she is my Sunshine." Jason voiced with excitement.

"How's Claire's drinking problem?" Catherine asked, with a concerned tone.

"Well, she's averaging two full bottles of wine per day that I know of, for sure. I'm hoping this cruise helps the family. Claire and I have some spa days scheduled for some much-needed adult time." Jason stated.

"How's Adam doing with his needs?" Catherine asked while jotting notes onto a legal pad.

"Well, the only way to keep him entertained so I can work is with videogames. I don't know what else to do, doc? He needs constant attention without them. I can't focus on work. His anxiety is way too out of control, and I'm running out of ideas. I hope the fresh air and constant outside entertainment, will keep him away from the videogames, and ease his anxiety some. Maybe then Claire and I can bring ourselves back together." Jason retorted with a hopeful tone.

"Jason, that's all the time we have for today, we'll pick up on our next session. Enjoy your vacation, and don't fret the things you can't control." Catherine said as she walked him out of her office.

CHAPTER 2

Emily Rogers was overlooking the ocean. She smiled, giggling into the phone. "I'm finally getting my dream wedding. Everything is perfect, Mom. I just got off the phone with the wedding coordinator on the ship; she has taken care of everything." Relief fell over her voice.

"What are you doing now, dear?" Her mother Maryann pried.

"I'm at the hotel on the balcony. Watching this amazing sunrise."

Satisfied her daughter was content. "Okay, honey, we will meet at the terminal at 7 am." Maryann said in a cheerful tone.

∞

"It's such a beautiful day," Katy the stewardess was saying, looking out the window of the ship. "The clouds are amazing."

"I know, it's always a beautiful day. Let's go over the itinerary." Debby said in an exhausted tone.

"Okay, Debby downer," Katy whispered with a sarcastic smirk.

"Let's see. We have one wedding onboard to set up

for; the bride chose the aft pool area for the ceremony. Captain McElroy will be doing the honors, and reception is to be at Chops grill as requested." Debby seemed pleased with the choices.

"How many guests are at the party?" Katy asked.

"22 and one puppy delivering the rings," Debby exclaimed with an unenthused look.

"Oh, that's so adorable." Katy giggled.

∞

Captain McElroy was sitting on the private balcony, a cool breeze blowing through his hair. He looked out over the dock, observing his crew loading provisions down below. Satisfied, he turned to his wife.

Patty was looking at the Captain. "After all these years, I still can't get enough of you, dear." She said with beaming eyes.

He smiled, pulled her close and said. "I love you too. We will be leaving for Belize at 9 am sharp. Is there anything you need from the town before we set off my love?"

"Just you," she stated with a playful voice.

He grabbed Patty, pulling her close and kissing her passionately.

∞

Claire was unhappy. It was another miserably hot humid day in Houston. The air was thick, with a faint petroleum smell that seemed never to go away. She was silently complaining to herself as she walked to the terminal, unable to bite her tongue any longer. "It's completely unbearable without air conditioning," she whined.

The sound of seagulls filled the air with a faint ship horn in the distance. "Welcome aboard," the crew was cheering, as the guest strolled through the passerelle onto the ship. Ariana was looking around in amazement, that was when her eyes met his. Brice looked at her with a smile in his eyes, as he watched her walk by. Ari couldn't help but blush at the shockingly handsome young man, taking an interest in her. She didn't feel she was much to look at, but the smile he gave her, instantly sent goosebumps down her spine.

Adam poked Ari in the side, teasingly, "Ariana has a boyfriend."

Ari snapped to attention, stopping abruptly and turning to face Adam, socking him in the shoulder for good measure. "You're lucky Mom and Dad didn't hear you, because I would end you," she scolded.

Adam's eyes widened, and he composed himself quickly. Satisfied, Ariana turned to catch up to their parents, followed by Adam rubbing his shoulder.

The cruise ship, of course, was the most luxurious available, but Claire found several things sadly lacking. Jason and the children tuned her out as she whined about everything from the lack of closet space in the cabins to the small showers they would be using. It didn't matter that the ship had shops and restaurants that were top of the line. It didn't matter that there were the best gym facilities and a selection of different pools. None of that mattered because Claire was never happy with anything. As a matter of fact, her husband believed deep inside that the sole purpose of her existence was to criticize and complain, and she did her job well.

Adam didn't let something like a cruise interfere with his gaming. He made sure to have a portable system and his smartphone with him at all times. The thought of actually communicating with his family for an extended period, may cause him to jump overboard. Instead, he focused on his wonderful devices and answered all questions with a yes or a no. He would offer up no more. Why put in any extra effort if you didn't have to?

Ariana, on the other hand, enjoyed mingling and getting to know people. Some had brought their pets, and she made the most of any time she had with them. She made fast friends with an older couple with a Pomeranian in hopes that they would allow her to 'babysit' their 'child' at some point during the cruise. In Ariana's opinion, that would have made the vacation perfect. She had her heart set on getting a small dog of her own, but so far, her mother had put a kibosh on all her attempts. Ari was patient, though; she would simply bide her time.

As for the Harrington's marriage, Jason and Claire simply tolerated each other. While they had been crazy for each other years ago, in the very beginning, the love had been slowly fading between them. They stayed together for the sake of the children, as Claire liked to tell her friends, but everyone knew it was only for the sake of appearances.

CHAPTER 3

Decker, the dog, loped down the dusty street. His head ached, and his belly growled. His tongue stuck to the roof of his mouth as if he had been eating peanut butter. Lately, Decker had been blessed with finding fresh food in the alley near the big brick building in town, and though the meat was not steak, it satisfied his taste for blood and the ravenous hunger which threatened to consume him. No matter how much he ate, he was always hungry. He could never get enough; he was never satisfied.

He was nearing the alley now, and the meal he was sure to find there: smelly rodents that the men in white coats brought out the side door and threw in the bin every day. They tossed them by the bag-full, and even though it consisted of dead rats, the dog wasn't about to complain. He was lucky to be getting anything to eat at all. 'Don't look a gift horse in the mouth' was his motto.

As he neared the entrance of the alley, which was blocked off on the other end, he looked up at the darkening sky; perhaps there would be rain today. It certainly appeared promising anyway. The sky was dark gray and very cloudy. He could sure use a drink to top off his meal. All he could do was hope. He was so thirsty.

Decker took a right into the alley just in time to see one of the men in white coats toss a knotted plastic bag at the bin. He missed, but that did not stop him from turning around and heading back inside, the door slamming shut behind him. The human could not even be bothered to make sure the garbage made it into the bin, but this was good news for Decker. It made his venture much more manageable. An eager whine escaped from his throat.

He picked up his pace once the door latched closed, and soon he was tearing at the bag with his ragged nails and stained, broken teeth. In no time, four rats were fully exposed, dead, blank looks on their faces. There was no blood, just dead bodies, and though Decker was able to detect an 'off' flavor about them, he didn't care and dug right in. All he knew was that they filled his belly, and to be honest, they weren't bad tasting, either.

Decker, ate eagerly, no sound coming from him but a light growl and the wet smacking of his jaw as he chewed now and then. He tore into the rat flesh that was his supper. He had been coming here for a couple of weeks eating the rodents every day, and while they satisfied him, he also had begun to feel progressively worse. His head and belly ached all the time, and Decker could feel the heat radiating from his eyes that made him nauseous. Sometimes, he even got the overwhelming urge to bite into a human and shake them into a bloody mess, but he had lived amongst people long enough to know that would be the end of him. He controlled his urges, and he escaped into solitude when the sounds of those living around him caused unbearable irritation.

As Decker ate, the rain began to fall, first in large, splashing drops, and then in torrents. He had one rat left, and though he was soaked through and through, he was determined to eat his fill. However now was the time to tuck his meal away, out of sight, and find a nice puddle to drink from. It would be easy, the way this rain was falling. Maybe he would finally be able to quench this terrible thirst.

Decker took the last rat in his mouth and hid it behind the bin amongst some dead leaves and sticks. Then he headed back toward the mouth of the alley to get a drink. Perhaps a good stomach full of water would ease the sharp pains he felt there, as well as relieve the pounding in his head that never seemed to go away.

The rain was monstrous, pouring down on him and around him. It was dark, and it was hard for him to see; the things he could see were visible only in the street lamps and the lights of oncoming cars. Decker staggered back and forth slowly and painfully, looking all around him as he did for a good puddle from which to drink.

He found a smaller puddle and began to lap out of it slowly. It hurt his head even worse to bend over and drink, but he squinted his black, bloodshot eyes against the pain and lapped away. Suddenly a human vehicle shot passed him, very close, blaring its horn loudly.

Decker jumped back and cowered, trembling and whining with startled fear. They didn't care. He knew if one of the human vehicles ever hit him, they likely would not even stop to see if he was okay. He had seen it time and time again.

The vehicle disappeared in the rain and darkness, and that was when Decker saw the giant puddle in the middle of the road, but just barely. The only reason it was visible was because of the rain hitting it and splashing upward. He wondered if the rain hurt the puddle when it hit, the way it pained him, through his coat. Each drop felt like he was being stabbed with a tiny knife over and over again.

Decker looked back and forth, checking for human vehicles before he made his way to the large puddle. He was filled with eagerness and dying of thirst, but he found he could only go so fast. Every joint in his body ached terribly, but the thirst drove him to the puddle's edge. He began to lap at the water, slowly but surely, shaking and trembling violently as he did so.

He drank, his tail began to wag with pleasure, hitting the wet pavement without sound. Decker no longer heard the things going on around him. He was so focused on the delicious chilled beverage. He wished he could gulp it, if only to be human, so he could put it in a glass and pour it down his throat, the way the two-legged ingrates did.

Suddenly the light was there, all around him, lighting up Decker and the puddle that served as his water bowl. He jerked his head up to look, but that was the last thing he knew. It was the headlights of a semi-truck, and it hit Decker full force on the passenger side, and every other tire on that side ravaged through his body in succession.

Decker, the dog, lived no more.

Roberto Perriera slammed on the semi's brakes as he approached the Belize testing facility, trying to avoid the big furry beast by the puddle, but by the time he even saw him, it was too late. He felt his semi tires hit the stray, and he knew that more than one tire had their way with the poor creature. He struggled with the steering wheel and finally brought the heavy vehicle to a full stop. Roberto sat behind the wheel for a moment, his heart pounding and his hands shaking violently.

"Damn," Roberto said, breathing in and out rapidly. When he had calmed himself a bit, he opened the door and jumped from the cab of the truck, both feet hitting the ground at once and splashing water everywhere. The rain was terrible, with limited visibility, especially with the truck's lights facing the opposing direction. He reached up and behind the driver's seat of the truck and pulled out a large black flashlight, which he turned on. He then began to shine the beam of light through the rain toward the large puddle. He wanted to see what he had hit and get it out of the road if he could.

He made his way toward a large dark mass, which he assumed was the animal he struck. It was not near the puddle's edge anymore. Instead, the truck had dragged it quite a distance. Yes, Roberto thought as his stomach lurched with a mix of nausea and sadness, this is what I hit. He had always been an animal lover, and it pained him every time he witnessed one that was hurt. This time, he had done the hurting, and he felt guilty.

He reached the pile of fur and shined his light down on it. The thing was soaked in water and blood, and it was mangled. Bones stuck out here and there, broken and crushed. The beast's head had been flattened to the point that one of its eyes hung out and lay on the pavement. Roberto closed his eyes and shook his head, then used the sleeve of his jacket to wipe the rain from his face. The critter, which he thought might be a dog, was undoubtedly dead.

He looked around him; no one was near. He couldn't bear the thought of just leaving the mess where it was. He didn't want the poor animal to be run over again and again. After all, it had been an accident, and Roberto had a reasonably soft heart. He took notice of an alleyway nearby, picking it up in his arms would definitely get blood all over him. Without so much as a second thought, he gave the beast's body a good hard kick. He would get it off the road by kicking it into the alley. It wasn't like it was feeling anything anyway.

The poor stray's body stuck to the ground at first, but with a second kick, it gave a slight ripping sound then gave. Roberto winced with disgust at the noise the carcass made, coupled with the feel of it against his foot. He blocked the sickness in his stomach, putting it out of his mind, and continued to kick the bloody corpse until it was just inside the alley and out of sight.

Satisfied, he went to the large puddle and stomped

in it for a bit, trying to clean the blood and fur from his boots. It was too dark to tell much, so he finally just returned to his truck and left. He put the thought of the animal's death out of his mind. What was done was done.

The rain continued to pour down on the streets, the buildings, and on Decker's body. His blood mingled with the water and ran onto the alleyway surface. The motionless dogs remains didn't move. It merely took the water as it came. Decker was dead.

Suddenly, his stomach began to rise; Decker had started to breathe! He could hear the rain falling again, and he could feel the intense pain in his joints and bones. His body jerked in response to the new life-force that was reanimating it. He was thirsty. If only he could peel himself off the concrete and get back to that puddle.

R.W.K. Clark

CHAPTER 4

As the massive ship cut through the water, Jason and Claire sat on the deck with colorful beverages and looked out at the ocean. Jason hated having to be alone with his wife. He always wound up listening to the silliness of the latest gossip, and he honestly couldn't care less.

"So, Michelle told me that she decided the best thing was to have an affair," Claire was telling him. "She feels it will teach Scott a valuable lesson. You know, if one can play, both can play."

"I don't care for either of them," Jason replied. "What do you want to do in Belize when we arrive?" He was trying to change the subject as quickly as possible. Who gives a darn about the marriage of Scott and Michelle Staton?

Claire got a surprised look on her face. "Shop, of course. What did you expect? Did you have other plans?"

"Would it matter if I did?" he asked, staring at the sea.

Now Claire finished her drink and motioned for the bartender to bring her another. "You can do what you want, Jason. You are going to anyway."

"You know what, Claire?" Jason began. "You went shopping four days ago. Then again, the day before yesterday. Do you know how many things there are to do in Belize? Of course, you do. But yet you want to 'go shopping.' It makes my stomach turn."

Claire laughed bitterly. "What doesn't make your stomach turn?" He made her sick. He had a beautiful wife, and never showed her the least bit of attention. He could just kiss her butt as far as she was concerned.

Jason rose with his drink and walked away from his wife. She was one of the most greedy, self-indulgent individuals he had ever met, and his son Adam was following in her footsteps. Jason could see him lounging at the nearby pool, but was he enjoying a good swim? No. He was playing some stupid damn video game. They could have just stayed at home and accomplished the same things. He and his delightful daughter should have come on the cruise alone. They could have truly enjoyed the vacation and all the exciting stuff Belize had to offer. Maybe they could take a trip together, just the two of them, next time around.

He walked up to the bar and finished his drink, setting the glass on the counter. "Another?" the bartender asked, and Jason replied with a nod and a tight smile. He would need one after another if he were going to survive this trip with the pain in the neck that called herself Mrs. Harrington.

So Jason resigned himself to the fact that they would dock in Belize and go shopping. There was no way around it because Claire would whine and complain if the three of them did not cooperate. She would put on a great big tearful show that consisted of the finest of guilt trips, in great detail about how no one ever wanted to spend time with her and do the things she wanted to do, how no one appreciated her. They would all end up giving in any way. It was best to acquiesce from the start and avoid the hassle that would ensue.

Jason took the fresh drink from the bartender and glanced up at the porthole-shaped clock on the wall. They would dock at Belize in one hour. He needed to talk to the kids and make sure they resigned themselves to participating in their mother's plans.

He went to Adam first, at the poolside. He sat next to his son and took a drink from his beverage. "How's it hanging? How's the game?"

Without looking up from the small screen or taking his fingers off the buttons of his portable game unit, Adam replied, "It's hangin' and the game rocks."

Jason sighed. "Will you put that thing down so I can talk to you for a minute? It will take only a sec."

Now Adam turned to his dad. "So which is it, Dad? A minute or a second?"

"Don't be a smartass, Adam," Jason said sternly, but he couldn't help but smile. His son was quick.

Adam sighed then, and paused the game, putting it on his lap. "What's up, Dad?"

"Well," Jason began, "We dock in Belize in an hour. I'm sure you had things you wanted to check out, but your mother insists we shop, so be prepared. It looks like we are going to be following her around and carrying shopping bags, Son."

Now Adam turned his body in full to his father, sitting up on the lounger rigidly. "Dad! All that woman wants to do is shop! If I have to shop, then I want to check out a new cell phone because mine is slowing down. Otherwise, I am not going."

Jason looked at the boy. How did this happen? How did he manage to marry someone like Claire and then create another one of the most selfish human beings on the planet? He gave a weary sigh. "Whatever, Adam. Just be ready." He stood and walked away. He wanted to find Ariana; if anyone could make him smile, it would be her. She was unquestionably his preferred child. While Adam tended to mirror Claire in attitude and behavior, Ari took after him.

He wandered the deck in search of his daughter, with no success. The ship was so big! He had told her to stay close, and she was not overly defiant. She was close by; he was sure. She was just mingling with the other passengers. Then he took the elevator to the upper deck. He had remembered she had made friends with an older couple named Strickland, and it seemed their cabin was upstairs.

He lit off the elevator and saw his daughter immediately. The sight of the sun shining off her long auburn hair made him smile. She was such a sweet girl, so easy to please, and never out for herself. Ariana was the light of her father's life. One look at her and all the problems he had with Claire and Adam disappeared like so much smoke.

He approached her, grinning from ear to ear. She had the small fluffy dog named Phu-fa-lou on her lap and was speaking with the dog's owner, an older lady named Lucy. "I'm sorry to interrupt you two girls," Jason said as he reached them. "I need to have a word with Sunshine here."

Ariana looked up and smiled at her dad. "Hi! Are you having fun yet?"

"A real blast," he replied, giving an exaggerated eye roll. "Can I speak to you alone? Only for just a moment?"

His daughter handed the Pomeranian to its owner, and then she linked her arm through her father's. "What's up, Pops?"

"We're docking soon," Jason said. "Your mother…"

Ariana cut him off, her smile fading. "Our mother wants to drag us all from shop to shop and spend money on useless items that she doesn't need and will never use."

Jason nodded. "Give that girl a prize!" He shook his head at his joke. "I just wanted to ask you to cooperate. I know you wanted to check out the local zoo, but she is determined."

"Oh, dad," the girl said. "She frustrates me terribly. You mean I won't be able to visit the zoo at all?"

Jason nodded. "She frustrates me too, but it will be much worse if we don't comply, dear. As for the zoo, well…" His words trailed off, then he continued. "I thought that for next vacation, we would let Mom and

Adam go together, and you and I could vacay. You know, two separate trips. What do you say?"

Ari's eyes lit up. "That sounds amazing! I know these trips are harder on you than any of us," she replied. "As for shopping, no problem, I guess. No problem at all."

Jason smiled. She was unique, his daughter. "So, you will meet us at the ramp in about a half-hour?"

"Of course." Ariana stood on her tiptoes and planted a kiss on her father's cheek. "Anything for you, Paw."

As she walked away and headed back to the Strickland's and their pooch, Jason watched her with a smile. If his marriage had any good points, it was Ariana. She made it all worth the frustration and misery, every second of it.

∞

The port in Belize proved to be a masterpiece of chaos and confusion. Three cruise ships in all, and passengers and tourists milled all around, bumping into each other and exchanging rude comments. Taxicabs were lined up near the port, up and down, both sides of the street. Drivers were waiting anxiously for someone, anyone, to hire them for their tourism excursions. People of all shapes, sizes, and colors hustled and bustled from here to there, the excitement on their faces visible.

Jason, Claire, and the children were standing near the taxis watching as people shoved their way to the cabs. Claire turned to Jason. "Well, aren't you going to do something? I'm certainly not going to walk to get my shopping done!"

"What would you have me do?" Jason asked.

Now she gave him an exasperated shrug. "I don't know; maybe get us a ride before all these other lowlife people get all the taxis?"

Just then, a low gravelly voice with a thick accent spoke, making Jason jump. "You need a taxi? Do you want shopping? Touring?"

All four of the Harrington's turned to the man speaking, who stood just near Jason on the other side. He was dirty, with greasy, stringy hair and shiny oil on his skin. His clothing was ragged and smudged with filth, and his teeth were rotting out of his skull. Claire could smell him, and the aroma made her gag. The man smiled at Jason, his yellowing eyes lighting up. "Taxi, yes?" he repeated in broken English.

Suddenly, Claire whispered at her husband, "I don't know. He's disgusting! Don't let him touch you!" She grabbed both Adam and Ariana by the arms and pulled them away from the stranger. Couldn't they get another taxi, one with a human being for a driver? She put her nose in the air and let Jason do the talking.

Jason turned back to the man and offered him a half-hearted smile. "Yes, we need a taxi," he said. "What can you offer us?"

The man bowed slightly at Jason and cleared his throat. "I will take you to shop all around the main street, up and down it. I will wait for you at the other end, and then I bring you back here to ship when you are done. This is good, yes?"

Jason had to take him up on the offer. Nearly all the other cabs were full, and to pursue one of the other empty ones might mean missing out altogether. He was not going to refuse a taxi just because the driver's hygiene was sadly lacking.

"Yes," he replied. "I think I will take you up on that."

Soon the four of them were in the cab and on the road. Claire and the kids in back and Jason next to the smelly man in the front. "See the street here?" the man asked. Without waiting for Jason to answer, he continued. "Shopping is all up and down both sides. Some expensive, but that no matter to you rich Americans, no?" He looked Jason over and cackled. "You shop all up the street, and I meet you right here." He parked the cab at the end of the strip. "Then I take you back to boat, yes? You have any questions. You need only to come and ask me; I will be right here."

Claire and the children were out of the backseat in no time, gasping for clean air. The man stank to high heaven, and Adam and Claire didn't miss an opportunity to make fun of the poor man together. Ari felt embarrassed by their immature behavior, and she refused to join in their reindeer games.

Jason paid the fare and gave the man a generous tip. "You will be here when we are done? If you are, there is more of this for you," he said, waving money at the driver.

"No problem," he said, his eyes growing wide at the

cash. "I will be here. I go nowhere!"

Finally, Jason got out of the cab with the rest of his family. With a wave to the driver, they were off. When they were out of earshot, Claire turned to Jason. "How could you stand to ride in the front with that stench all around you? I was simply dying in the backseat. Dying!"

"You know, Claire, the way you and Adam judge other people, one would think you both excrete rose petals. Well, I've got news for both of you: I've seen and smelled your bum, and rose petals have nothing to do with it!"

Ari laughed at her father's joke while Claire put her nose up as usual. What did her husband know? He never did appreciate her and the good wife she was to him.

The shopping finally began to get underway. The family visited one store after another, and both Claire and Adam managed to make purchases at each and every one. Ariana seemed to have no interest in anything, and Jason had to practically force her to choose something from the second to last shop. She picked a globe with dolphins in it, and when it was shaken, golden glitter swirled around in the water inside.

What Jason and Ari mostly did was carry bags and packages, trudging along behind Claire and Adam, listening to them talk about spending even more money at the next place, whatever that would be. Their selfish behavior was a private joke to Jason and his daughter, and their silent joking made the shopping trip much more bearable.

The day passed very quickly. Before they knew it, they were standing at the last shop, a small boutique situated across the alley from a large, official-looking brick building. They would check the shop out, spend money pointlessly, and then finally make their way back to the stinky man in the smelly cab. The misery was almost over.

But at the last shop, both Ariana and Adam had enough of the shopping. Claire was taking her sweet time browsing through the clothing, jewelry, and other trinkets, and the kids had grown excessively bored. They were both ready to get back to the ship and give their legs a rest. Adam planted himself on a bench just outside the door and pulled his smartphone from his pocket to play a game. "I can't wait to get my new phone set up. It's top of the line, you know," he said smugly to his sister. "Why did you only get a stupid snow globe? You could have anything you want anytime, idiot. You are Dad's favorite, you know."

"Because I don't need anything," she replied with aversion. "Plus, nothing else caught my eye, and it is silly to think I'm Dad's favorite; he loves us both the same."

"Ha!" he replied. "I know I'm Mom's favorite, and I don't mind saying it."

Ari began to pace back and forth. "What is taking her so long? What could she possibly be buying that she doesn't already have?"

Adam laughed sarcastically. "You know Mom," he said, then focused his attention back on his game.

Ariana sat next to him, swinging her legs back and forth and observing all the people around them. Suddenly, from somewhere behind her, Ariana heard what sounded like a whimpering baby. She jerked her head toward the sound and tried to block out all the chaos around her. There it was again!

The second whimper and all those that followed sounded very needy and persistent. It was certainly an animal of some sort. "Adam, do you hear that? It sounds like a dog." She stood up and stared down the alleyway. "It sounds like a stray that has been hurt."

"Hear what?" he snapped at her. "I don't hear anything. Don't you see I'm busy? Damn, I just died because of you!"

She began to walk toward the alley that ran between the buildings. She stopped at the opening and looked down the length of it. There were large garbage bins, and garbage littered all through the walkway. At the very end of the alley, something moved, and she heard the whimper again. Yes, it was undoubtedly an animal, and she was willing to bet it had been hurt.

"What are you doing?" Adam's voice was a bit urgent. Suddenly, he was right next to her, and he took hold of her hand. "You need to stay with me. I don't want mom and dad to jump my case because you won't sit still."

Ariana jerked her arm free of her brother's grasp. "There is an animal down there crying," she said, glaring at him. "I'm just going to check on it; come with me if you want, but I'm going no matter what." With that, she entered the narrow opening. It bothered her to no end that her brother thought he could dictate what she did. Sure, her parents had told her to stay with Adam, but all she had to do was watch him. He didn't care, so he needed to mind his own business.

Adam watched her for only a moment, then ran to catch up. I'm not going to be the one to catch a lecture from the parents, he thought to himself.

The two slowly approached the animal, and as Ari neared it, she could tell it was a dog. Its whimpering was growing louder, and she was sure the stray was hurt. Her heart swelled with compassion, and she picked up her pace. At about five feet from it, Ari crouched down and held out her hand. The creature sniffed in her direction and then continued to whimper painfully.

Yes, Ari was willing to bet that the mangled, bloody mess before her was a dog, but for the life of her, it sure did not look like one. Its legs were broken and going in strange, unnatural directions. Its head was caved in on one side, and one of its ears was ripped almost all the way off. Patches of fur were missing, and the bald spots in its coat showed ashy-colored flesh with purple veins standing out in stark contrast. The mutt looked as if it should be dead.

But it was not.

"That's disgusting," Adam spat with disgust.

Her heart got the better of her. She crawled to the animal on her hands and knees until she was right next to it. One of its back legs looked to be broken in at least three places; the poor beast had to be in terrible pain!

Its fur was matted with blood and dirt, and one of its eyes seemed to be missing. While the other eye was so black she could not see the white at all, giving the pup an evil look, as if the devil possessed it. She cringed a bit at the thought but pushed the worries from her mind. For goodness sakes, Ari, she thought to herself, it's just a stray. A poor, injured, sick pet.

"Are you okay, little one?" Ariana spoke softly as she timidly began to stroke the animal gently with the back of her hand. How could she help the beast? She would have to walk away, she knew, but her heart broke at the thought. After all, they were on a cruise, and even if they weren't, her parents would never let her take the dog in. It was in terrible shape. Her father would want to put it out of its misery right then and there. The thought made her sick.

Adam kneeled to join Ariana and put his hand out slowly so the creature could smell him.

"Ariana!" Her mother's voice snapped at her from the mouth of the alleyway. "What are you doing? What do you have there?"

The girl jumped at the sound and turned toward her mom. The dog was startled as well, and suddenly he snapped at Adam, catching his skin on its teeth. Adam cried out, and the stray continued to whimper. He looked down at his hand to see a small, bleeding scratch. It would be okay; it was nothing more than a slight surface wound Adam thought to himself.

"Poor baby," she said to the dog, then to her mother she said, "It's a stray, Mom. We're coming now!"

Adam brought his hand to his mouth and licked the blood away. It wouldn't do for their parents to see that the mutt had bitten him.

Adam pleaded, "Don't tell Mom she will freak out, please Ari just a bandage."

Ariana was studying her brother's face. "Okay, okay, calm down."

Their dad would likely bash its head in if he found out. She petted the dog again and said, "I'm sorry. I have to go. I hope you are going to be okay." A couple of tears fell from her eyes, and she quickly brushed them away. Couldn't let them see her crying over something like this. Her mother and brother would poke fun at her over it for the next month. She mumbled a quick prayer for the injured animal under her breath.

With that, she stood, and the two went to meet there family. After letting her mother holler at her for a moment about not staying close, she took some of the shopping bags from her dad and helped him carry them to the cab. While her mother and brother walked together, arms empty, Ariana and her father bore the load.

The cab and driver were sitting right where they had left it, just as the driver had promised. He was napping when they arrived, but they were able to wake him quickly. He jumped from the driver's seat and helped Jason and Ari put the packages in the vehicle's trunk, then they all got back in the cab and headed out.

Getting back to the ship would be good. The heat of

Belize seemed to be making Adam a bit queasy. He could use something cold to drink and a nap.

As they entered the ship, Ari looked at Adam. "We will go to the infirmary, come on." The two made their way to the elevators. Soon they were at the medical office.

"Could my brother get some help he has a small cut?" Ariana said as she looked at the handsome young man that stood before her. She was desperately trying to divert her eyes, as not to be so obvious.

"Hi, I'm Brice, the ship's Doctor, what happened here?" Brice asked in a soothing voice.

"It's just a scratch," Adam said in a matter of fact tone.

"Okay, well, let me clean it and dress the wound," Brice said, smiling at the two of them. "Follow me."

The exam room was bright, with a sterile smell of cotton balls. Ariana could feel the blood rushing to her cheeks as she looked around and smiled.

Brice walked out for supplies, and Adam looked at Ari with a grin. "You like him... Ari's got a boyfriend." Adam teased.

"Stop it, brat." She spat with fire in her eyes. Adam instantly stopped and corrected his posture, patiently waiting for the doctor to return.

I'm in college now, and on a cruise ship, Ariana pondered as she looked at herself in the mirror while touching up her lip gloss. It's time to stretch my wings and have a little fun. She thought as she snapped the lid to her lip gloss closed.

Yes, that fiery redhead was up to no good. What could possibly go wrong they were in the middle of the ocean?

Within moments, Brice entered the room with antiseptic and a bandage. Instantly Ariana felt her temperature rising as she watched him tend to her brother. Nonchalantly Ari tried to fan herself with a magazine in an attempt to soothe her heart. What's wrong with me, she thought to herself?

"Adam, you're all set," Brice said, breaking Ariana's trance. Content, Adam finally left the room as Ari lingered just long enough to talk with Brice.

"So, have you been enjoying your vacation?" Brice asked.

"Yes, I love the fresh air, and I can't believe how big this ship is," Ariana said in an excited tone. She was thrilled to have a one on one conversation, finally. Could this be real, am I dreaming? She thought while contemplating to pinch herself. "How about you give me a personal tour later?" She asked cheerfully.

"I've never given a tour before," Brice said, flattered by the question.

"Oh come on, you can break the rules for me," Ariana said, smiling. Either way, she had the hots for him and was not taking no for an answer.

Brice thought to himself, wow, it was nice to meet a confident woman, brave enough to ask him out first. He never experienced anything of the sorts: my, my how the tables have turned.

"So, tonight is my birthday dinner with my parents

how about after?" She offered as her eyes met his with a smile.

"Perfect, let's meet in the solarium at 10 pm?" Brice offered. He was intrigued by the situation and looking forward to seeing Ariana later.

Suddenly there was a tap on the door as it opened, a nurse hastily peaked in her head. "Doctor, we need you in exam room B, please." The nurse stated in an urgent voice.

Ariana agreed to meet him later then swiftly left the exam room, the conversation playing back in her mind. Her proposition slid out of her mouth in an instant, she wondered, did she seem too eager? Regardless Ari was pleased to get to know Brice on a personal level. Giddy with excitement, she made her way to the elevator.

R.W.K. Clark

CHAPTER 5

"A doctor, that's my girl," Claire said with a smile from ear to ear.

"Mom!" Ariana's voiced shocked at her mother's comment.

"What honey? Be honest, think about it. For example, how is some meager security guard going to take care of my daughter's needs?" She prattled while primping her daughter's hair. "Now, a doctor, bravo!" Claire said with an exaggeratedly happy tone.

Her mother could be so rude, insinuating she just likes Brice because he is a doctor. Stunned at her mother's comment, Ariana snapped. "No, mom, he is smart and sexy, hello." Shooing her mother's hand away from her hair, while rolling her eyes at her insinuations.

"Yes honey and rich, now, help me with my dress." Claire expressed while turning her back to Ariana.

Mentally defeated, Ariana helped zip her mother's dress while thinking. Why is life so complicated at times? Am I becoming my mother?

Regardless Ariana was excited about her date with the dashingly handsome doctor.

Adam lay in the bunk in his cabin. He felt exhausted, and he had a terrible headache. Man, that little trip into Belize had taken a lot out of him. Adam felt like all he wanted to do was sleep, but no matter how hard he tried, he could not cross into dreamland.

There was a light knock on his door. "Adam?" It was his dad's voice. "Can I come in?"

"Yeah, Dad. Come on in," he replied, and the sound of his voice made his head pound even harder. It wore him out just to answer him.

His father entered and sat on the bunk next to him. "How are you feeling?"

"Yucky," he told him and offered the best smile he could muster. "Maybe I ate something bad. I don't know, but I feel miserable. My head hurts something awful, and I think I have a fever."

Jason held the back of his hand to his forehead. "You're burning up, child!" He stood and said, "I'll be right back. I'm going to get some medicine so we can bring your fever down."

He was gone only a minute, returning with two pills and a glass of water. As he took them, Jason asked, "What would you like me to bring you to eat? I'm sure you don't want to join us."

"You're right," he replied. "But the thought of food is making my stomach turn, Dad." He closed his eyes and put a hand over them. "If you insist, you can just bring me soup or something maybe, and a glass of apple or orange juice would be nice, Please."

Jason pulled the blankets over him and tucked them in around his body. "That's fine. You just stay here and get some rest. I'm sure there was just too much excitement for one day, and that you will feel better soon."

His dad left, and as soon as he heard his cabin door latch shut, he turned on the small lamp next to his bunk. He held his hand up to the light, as he took his bandage off and looked at it closely. The bite mark was so red it was nearly purple, and it looked like a bit of puss was forming around the wound. Adam went into the bathroom, where he washed his hand thoroughly. It was so painful! Then he put a bit of ointment on it and wrapped it in a hand towel.

He felt a bit of confusion about the bite. It had only been a surface scratch, barely anything at all. It hadn't even hurt that much at the time. But now it was pulsating with pain, and it looked deep and infected. It made no sense to him whatsoever.

He lay back down and closed his eyes. He was so tired! It would be great if he could just fall right to sleep. He let his mind wander, and soon rest took over, supplying him with disturbing dreams of whimpering, bloody dogs with broken legs and sharp teeth.

∞

"So," Claire began when Jason came back to their table. "I take it your little brat will not be joining us this evening?"

Jason gave his wife a disgusted smirk. "Your sarcasm does not escape me, Claire," he said. "This is your son you are condescending about, and no, Adam is not joining us. He is sick. He has a fever." He sat down and then continued. "Any other mother in the world would be concerned, but I notice you couldn't care less, or so it appears."

"Well, then, I guess we will just order something to take to him later," she replied, embarrassed at his confrontation.

He nodded. "He asked for a simple soup and either apple or orange juice. I'll take care of it."

The three then went about ordering and eating their food. Ariana could barely pull her attention away from the thought of seeing Brice later tonight long enough to take a bite now and then. As for Claire, she kept looking in her compact mirror and fixing her already flawless makeup. While Jason kept worrying about his son. He had been fine all morning. If he weren't better by tomorrow, he would take him to visit the ship's doctor.

When dinner was over, Jason took a tray with a bowl of chicken noodle soup and a glass of orange juice to his son's cabin. He rapped lightly, and when he got no response, he opened the door to darkness.

"Adam, I brought you some soup," he said. Adam stirred slightly but offered no response. He entered and reached to the left to turn on the bathroom light. The main light would surely disturb him, and if he was sleeping, that was the last thing he wanted to do.

When he got to his bed, he set the tray on the nightstand. His son was in a ball under the blankets, nothing but his hair sticking out. He reached down to touch his forehead and check his temperature; he was cold! Well, he thought, at least the fever had broken.

That was when Jason noticed the smell.

It was coming off of his body in waves, and it reeked of black rot. Jason jerked his head back to get away from it. Whatever he had eaten that had made him sick was apparently bad; Adam was expelling some horrendous gas that was for sure. Yes, he was going to take him to see the ship's doctor first thing in the morning.

Once again, he tucked his blankets around him, noting that he didn't stir in the slightest at his touch. He would let him be for the night, and if he weren't feeling better by morning, he would deal with it appropriately, fever or no fever. He then kissed his hand and held it to his son's head before leaving the room.

As he walked back to his cabin, he thought of his wife. Never had he known a woman in his life that showed such little regard for one of her children, especially when that child was ill. Claire acted as though she didn't care that Adam was sick at all. He knew she wasn't the most compassionate mother, and the two didn't have the ideal mother-son relationship, but how could she not be bothered with her child? He found he disliked his wife more and more with each passing day. She had changed so much over the years.

They had begun dating in high school. Jason remembered her to be the cutest little thing, with a wonderful sense of humor and quick wit. She used to volunteer at one of the homeless shelters in Houston back then. She had goals, dreams, and ambitions. He couldn't wait to marry her.

But somewhere along the line, she had changed. If he gave it enough thought, he would be able to pinpoint precisely when the changes began to come over her. It started when he experienced success in his business. Yes, he was sure of it; the changes in Claire had a direct link to their money, and he found he despised the entire situation.

∞

After dinner, Ariana stood on the balcony of her stateroom. Prior to her date with Brice. I never imagined air smelling so clean, she thought to herself. A cool breeze sweeping over the deck, and with a long deep breath, Ari let out a sigh of relief. "Paradise simply paradise," she murmured. The moon peeking through the clouds was astounding like a photograph coming to life, simply unbelievable. Perhaps oceanography would be a better field than veterinarian school? The thought clouded her mind. I could get used to this real fast, poking at her frozen drink with the umbrella toothpick. She was smiling as she took a sip and began to read her book.

Right then, Ariana's stateroom phone began to echo loud, she answered. Her brother's voice broke through, disrupting her book and breaking her concentration. The fact that it was her little brother pissed her off even more. The little brat knew not to bother her unless it was a life or death situation. The chances that he would be disrupting her reading were always high, and she was going to tear into him for doing it this time. She squinted her eyes at her book, sitting next to her. Yep, she was going to have to give him a severe talking to, that was for sure.

"What is it now?" she asked him. "You just interrupted my book. I think we have had this conversation over and over again!"

Adam replied, "I need you to bring me something to drink. My stomach is upset."

"Go get it yourself, brat. All you have to do is call room service," his sister told him and prepared to hang up.

He growled into the phone, "If you don't, I will tell dad, and he will take your new book, I promise. I don't feel like waiting a half an hour or more for someone to bring me a drink. I'm thirsty right now."

Ariana's eyes narrowed; way to pull strings, brat, she thought to herself. "Do you have a frog in your throat? Why do you sound so funny?"

"I'm sick, idiot! Are you going to help me out or not?"

Ariana jumped slightly. He sounded mean, and even a bit violent. "Fine. I'll be there in a minute. Is soda okay?"

"Whatever," he said, and then the receiver went dead in her hands.

She proceeded to walk to the pool area. As she navigated her way around the edge of the pool, she got the attention of the steward. "Could you please bring me a soda to go?"

"Right away, miss," the man replied, and went to fetch the beverage.

He better appreciate me, the little punk, Ari thought to herself. She usually didn't take threats well, but she believed his threats when it came to Dad. They both knew he preferred Ari, just as Mom preferred Adam. But, Dad was still fair to them both when it came to discipline.

Soon she was making her way to her brother's cabin, soda in hand for the little twerp.

"Adam, open up! It's Ari. I have your soda." The young woman stood outside her brother's stateroom, waiting for him to let her in. Her foot tapped impatiently as she waited. What the heck was taking the little brat so long, anyway? "C'mon, Adam, open the door!"

Shortly, she heard the lock click on the other side. She waited for her brother to open the door, but he did not. "Hello? Are you going to open up?"

"It's unlocked," Adam said in a low voice. She could barely hear him. "What the hell are you waiting for?"

She raised her eyebrows at his use of a curse word, then Ari turned the handle and pushed gently on the door. The room was pitch black, and it reeked like stinking rot. She reached up to the left and flipped the light switch. Suddenly the room lit up.

She looked at the empty bed. "Adam?"

There was no one in the cabin. Ari let the door swing shut behind her and walked into the adjoining bathroom. She turned on that light, but he was not in there either.

"Stop playing damn games," she hollered.

The bathroom was a mess. There was even what appeared to be drops of blood on the tile. Ariana stared at the scene, her mouth wide open. Was Adam okay? Where was he, anyway?

She backed slowly out of the bathroom, reaching to turn off the light when he grabbed her from behind. It all happened so fast. Ariana didn't even have time for her mind to register what was going on, or even scream. "You brat," she jumped, her heart was pounding through her chest. "Here is your soda, jerk!" socking him in the arm for good measure.

∞

As Jason lay in bed that night, he worried terribly about his son until sleep came. It eluded him for some time, and Jason tossed and turned. More than once, he thought about getting up and checking in on him, but he talked himself out of it every time. Adam needed to rest if he was going to get well and enjoy the rest of the cruise. He would leave him alone.

When sleep did come, his dreams frightened him. He dreamed an evil dog had attacked his son while he stood by helplessly and watched. He managed to fight the animal off in the dream, but when he came to his son, he had changed. He attacked him, eating the flesh off his bones and laughing at his pain. He woke with a start and sat up straight in his bed, his heart pounding violently. He was covered in his sweat.

In the dream, his son was already dead, and there

was nothing he could do to help him; he was far too late.

∞

The solarium was fabulous, sporting a bright moon and a cool breeze with merely a hand full of people, including the two love birds, making the location the perfect choice for a fantastic evening.

"I'm into sharpshooting. I've been competing since I was 10. I've always had a steady hand. Enough about me tell me about you. How did you get to be a Doctor on a cruise ship?" Ariana asked, taking a sip of her drink.

"Well, that's a tough subject. I guess I wanted to disappear for a while." Brice paused for a bit, then continued. "I was interning on my final days before getting hired on full-time, and I had a patient my age with complications. To make a long story short. The primary said it was out of my control. But I feel responsible like I could have done more." Ariana locked eyes with Brice with a concerned look on her face as she waited for him to continue. "I would have to say I feel accountable to this day. I don't like talking about it, how about we get started with that tour?" He asked.

Brice's tour was nothing less than amazing. He took her to see the bridge, and she could hardly believe her eyes. This massive luxurious passenger ship was utterly unbelievable. The navigation system had autopilot with every bell and whistle; it could pilot itself around the world. The cherry on top was the ships weather station, Ari was sure it would rival the local news channels back home.

∞

Ariana walked into the bridge, looking around in amazement, "wow, this is incredible," she said with a bewildered expression.

Brice turned to Ariana with a smile, "Captain, this is Ariana."

Captain McElroy took Ariana's hand in his and kissed it. "It's a pleasure to meet you, Ariana. Perhaps Brice will show you the employee lounge and introduce you to more of the crew later." Captain McElroy paused, turning his attention back to the ship. He flipped some switches on the console, then turned back to Ariana and continued, "the crew likes to unwind before bed. Although, I am afraid I will not be there, as I'm an early riser. You two kids have fun." He said in his hardy voice.

"Thank you, Captain," Brice said with a smile as he watched McElroy leave the bridge. Brice turned to Ariana, "shall we continue the tour?" He said as he offered his arm to her, securing it tightly in his while they left the bridge.

During the elevator ride, Brice turned to Ariana and said, "there is one last place I would like to show you before we head to the employee lounge for drinks."

The excitement in Ariana's eyes grew, "okay!" she exclaimed. She was having a fantastic time. The elevator door opened, and they walked down the hall, passing some crew quarters. The corridor was quiet and void of all the fancy décor. Finally, the two approached a sizeable mechanical door that looked to be watertight. Brice reached for a lever, and as he pulled it, the hydraulic locks rattled and clicked, and the door began to open with an audible beeping sound.

"What's that noise?" Ariana questioned, with apprehension.

"That's just the warning that the door is moving and to stay clear," Brice said soothingly.

They entered the engine control room, where Ariana met the chief engineer and his crew. After a bit, the pair made their way to the employee lounge. It was late, and the private after-party was in full swing. The rest of the passengers were not privy to such a treat. She felt honored to join in on the festivities. Ariana was ready to enjoy some drinks and mingle with the crew.

Never in Ariana's life had she connected with a person as she did with Brice, they were at ease with each other instantly as if they knew one other for years. From completing each other's sentences to knowing what the other was thinking. They giggled and laughed all night long.

While Brice loved everything about her from her soft voice, and tinder heart, to her outgoing personality and thirst for knowledge.

Their evening was terrific. Ariana was indeed falling head over hills for this dashingly handsome compassionate man. No boy had ever treated her, the way he did, if she was ever asked, she would say it was the best six hours of her life.

CHAPTER 6

Adam rose from his bed at the break of dawn. He had no recollection of where he was or even who he was. His mind was a complete blank. All he knew was that he was ravenously hungry and thirsty, and the cravings he was having were for all things fresh.

He stood and went into the bathroom, where he looked at his reflection in the mirror. He was confused; who was he and what was he doing here? He reached out and touched the mirror as if to caress his cheek, but all he felt was the glass. With a grunt and a knit brow, he pushed on the mirror, trying to touch the person that stood in front of him, with very little success. Finally, in his frustration, he drew back and punched it, shattering the glass. Bits of his skin fell into the sink, but he didn't bleed, and he certainly felt no pain.

The person in the mirror had stringy hair that had no shine or waves. There were dark circles under his eyes that were completely black, and the surrounding skin was pasty white with purple blotches here and there. He growled a bit at the broken reflection in the mirror, then he pulled back and hit it with his fist again, shattering the glass even more. Unexpectedly, he was distracted by a loud rumbling in his stomach. He was hungry, and he needed to feed as soon as possible.

It was cold in the cabin, so cold Adam could hardly stand it. He sat back down on his bed, a persistent growl escaping his throat. His mind knew no words right away, only pictures, and now he thought of a woman with perfect makeup and blonde hair that was coiffed to perfection. The woman had been his mother in another life, a life that no longer existed.

That woman was Claire, and Adam was sure this woman would taste delicious.

He rose, holding his blanket tightly around him, and left the cabin. It was time for him to see what the blonde woman would be willing to feed him. He smiled as he made his way up the hall to his parents' stateroom. Willing or not, he was going to get a taste of her. The thoughts going through his mind made him chuckle, if jerky raspy breathing was indeed a chuckle. In his case, it was.

He reached the door to his parents' cabin. In his present state of mind, he was not identifying it as such. He just knew that the blonde woman he was looking for was on the other side of the door. He could smell her, and the smell was captivating. He was going to enjoy this meal to the fullest. He put his hand on the lever and began to turn it.

∞

Bruce West sat at his desk at the BioSearch testing facility in Belize. He had moved here with Dr. Jonathan Anson and the rest of the team when the experiments they were conducting, which had been outlawed in the States, were nearly discovered. It had proven to be a good move. Just last week, they had chanced upon a significant breakthrough in life after death, and it had taken only about a thousand rats to see real, tangible results.

Dr. Anson had begun the actual testing phase almost immediately after the move to Belize. It consisted of injecting rats with the serum he had created. Both Bruce and the doctor had spent all their waking moments monitoring and recording notes. There hadn't been too much to log in the early days. However, the rats always ended up dying before the first week was up.

Some considered his boss, Dr. Anson, to be a madman. Bruce did as well. But none of that mattered. What did matter was the high level of consequence that Bruce suspected everyone was going to pay for their experiments.

Dr. Anson theorized that the altering of a specific DNA strand would result in immortality. They had tried and failed countless times, which served to turn Anson's theory into an obsession. Just days ago, Bruce had thrown out a batch of mice from the final failure.

That night, Dr. Anson left the lab, seething with anger and frustration. It had been raining torrents, and Bruce had implored the doctor not to go until the storm let up, but the doctor ignored him, raging around the lab gathering his notes, laptop, and other essentials he would need to work at home.

Bruce had decided to come in early today. Perhaps if

he went through the records on the last batch of tests, a lightbulb would go off. It would surely be in his favor, so he dove in and began to review their notes.

∞

Claire sat at the vanity in the bathroom of her suite, applying her perfect makeup to her flawless face. Jason was such a jerk. He simply couldn't wait for her to get ready for breakfast. No, he would instead go and eat without her. Her mother had been right when she said Jason was worthless and she would regret marrying him. She regretted it every day. What had she ever seen in him?

Well, he had taken care of the family fine, and still did. They were worth millions, and even though it was shallow and she knew it, which was the only reason she stayed. Her mind went back to high school and how madly in love with him she had been back then—just a foolish young girl who didn't know what was right for her.

She began to apply powder to her face to set her makeup when she heard the door to her cabin rattling.

"Jason, is that you?" Claire called out, smiling to herself. Once again, she had won. He was such a simpleton. All it took for her to get her way, was to put on her fuss face and let him have a few whines. It worked every time. After all, here he was, fetching her for breakfast.

She received no response, which made her knit her brow. Was he trying to turn the tables on her by giving her the silent treatment? She peeled her ears and listened carefully; she heard the latch on the cabin door click as it closed, followed by a slight rustling.

"Jason?" Claire stood up from her place at the vanity and headed to the cabin's main area. As she walked, she attempted to put an earring in, and just before Claire reached the bathroom door, she heard the entrance to the stateroom open yet again, followed by Jason's voice.

"Claire, are you going to get over yourself and join me or not?"

She entered the cabin, a confused look on her face. "Did you just come in a moment ago and then leave?"

"What?" Jason asked. "No, I just got here."

Claire was more confused than ever. "I could have sworn…" she said, her voice trailing off. "Well, never mind. Yes, I suppose I will come with you."

She grabbed her purse from a chair next to the bed and took Jason's arm. He planted a kiss firmly on her cheek. "I wish you didn't have to be so disagreeable, dear," he told her. "It would make for a much better time if you weren't."

Claire smirked at him, and the two of them left the room to have their breakfast with their daughter. As far as Jason knew, Adam was still resting. He would check on him after the meal when he brought him something to eat.

Adam stood in the closet of his parents' cabin, watching his father kiss his mother. His breathing was labored and ragged, and as they left, he felt the rage building up inside of him. There goes my meal, he thought to himself, and he growled as he reached out to open the door all the way.

His movements were forced and jerky, moving from the closet to the bathroom, as everything was stiff. He looked at himself in the vanity mirror and thought he looked like death. His right eye was becoming a milky white over the iris, and he had purple patches and veins appearing all over his flesh. It didn't bother him, though. It seemed right. He might look lousy, but he felt like a million bucks. He felt invincible and powerful, and it felt good.

Adam had to feed. He felt if he didn't get some kind of nourishment, he would simply die, and he wasn't in the mood for eggs or cereal. No, Adam wanted something richer, something with more substance, something that bled.

He left the suite, lurching as he walked. He looked to the left and the right. That was when he saw a large red-haired woman at the end of the corridor looking over the railing at the sea. She wore a big yellow dress with bright red flowers all over it. Her arms were crossed over the handrail, which appeared to be supporting most of her weight. She was humming a light, airy tune to herself, and the sound made Adam's head pound.

Adam smiled lazily and turned toward her. He began to lurch clumsily in the woman's direction, and before he got even five feet away, he was overwhelmed with the woman's strong perfume. It made him gag, which frustrated him. Adam hoped it didn't affect the way the woman tasted.

As he neared the woman, Adam spoke, his voice guttural and forced. "Hello."

The woman turned toward Adam, and her eyes grew wide. What was wrong with the child before her? He looked terribly sick!

"My dear," the woman said, turning to Adam in full. "Are you feeling okay? You look ill, dear!"

Adam continued to close the gap between them. He held his arms up as if to ask for help. The woman rushed toward him as fast as her thick legs could carry her. "My name is Patty, dear. What can I do to help you? Where are your parents? Can I fetch your parents for you?" The woman continued forward, and when she reached him, she took him by the arms, as if to hold the boy up and steady him.

Then Adam grabbed the woman's arms in return, getting a good grasp on them, and there was plenty to hold. He felt so strong, and the woman seemed so weak. He leaned into her, and as the woman returned her embrace, Adam buried his face in the luscious neck and sank his teeth into her savory flesh. The woman tried to scream, but panic kept her from it, closing her throat immediately. After a minor struggle, she lay at the mouth of the corridor, her right foot twitching uncontrollably, her eyes and mouth wide with shock. There was a gaping hole in her neck, and blood was shooting out of it like a fountain.

Adam looked to the left and then the right. The corridor was empty. To his right, he saw a door marked 'Maintenance,' and he smiled. Perfect. His luck seemed to be smiling on him today.

Adam stood and took the woman by the wrists. Then he dragged the dead weight of her bloody body to the door. With a minor struggle, he was able to pull the body into the large closet and close the door behind them. There Adam sat, cross-legged, next to the woman, who was bleeding out from the neck before his very eyes. The fountain of blood had subsided to nothing more than an ooze now; the woman was indeed dead. He ran his hand through the woman's blood and brought it to his mouth, where he tasted it and smeared it all over his lips.

Delicious.

Without hesitation, he bent over and began to eat with wet, smacking sounds.

Breakfast was served.

CHAPTER 7

"Did either of you look in on Adam yet?" Ariana was sitting with her parents having a breakfast of steak and eggs. Jason and Claire seemed particularly affectionate, which was unusual and made her uncomfortable. She was trying to distract them from each other before their behavior made her puke up what she had eaten. This was no behavior to display at the dining table. What the heck was wrong with these people?

"You two need to take it to your cabin. For crying out loud," Ariana said with a disgusted tone.

Jason turned his attention to his daughter. "No, Sunshine, I haven't checked on Adam yet," he replied. "I plan to take him some bacon and juice when we are finished. I want to let him get as much rest as possible. I'm telling you when I saw him last night, he was burning up, and the next time he was ice cold, so the fever broke. He needed rest."

"I'm sure he is fine," Claire chimed in. "He is probably experiencing a spot of seasickness, I would assume. I would be willing to bet it is nothing more than that."

Jason nodded, rolling his eyes in disbelief. "You're likely right, but I want to offer him something, whether he eats it or not." He looked at Ariana again. "Have you gotten to see the entire ship yet?"

The girl reached for her napkin, wiping her mouth to speak. "Yep. This thing is a technological miracle. You wouldn't believe all the stuff it can do, and some of the available amenities are mind-boggling as well. It's going to be a blast getting to know it."

"I'm sure I would be impressed," Claire said, rolling her eyes at her daughter. "What are your plans today, Ariana, besides exploring the ship?"

Ariana offered her mother a sarcastic smirk. "I figured I would hang out on a float in the pool," she said. "Later, I will be dog sitting for the Strickland's."

Claire was rolling her eyes again as she spoke. "I just think you could spend a little time doing something beneficial."

Ariana laughed loudly. "You're one to talk, aren't you?"

A waiter appeared then. "More coffee?"

Jason held up his cup. "Could I also get a medium orange juice and two sides of bacon to go, please?"

"Right away, sir," the waiter replied. "Can I get anyone here anything else?"

Claire shook her head and wiped her mouth with her napkin. "No, thanks. I think we're good."

When the bacon and juice finally came, Jason stood. "I'm going to go check on Adam and offer him this food." He turned to Ariana. "Your mother and I are planning on getting massages in an hour. We will be spending most of the day at the spa. That's where we'll be if you need us." He bent down and kissed his wife.

"I'll meet you there, dear," Claire replied, winking at her husband.

With that, Jason left to take his son some food and see if his condition had improved. He certainly hoped he was feeling better.

∞

Adam stood at the deep sink in the maintenance closet. He had finished his wonderful, fresh meal and was just getting ready to leave the closet when something told him to clean up. It wouldn't do to wander around this big boat covered in blood, now would it?

Adam stood there, rinsing the blood down the drain, the body of Fatty Patty on the floor at his feet. Half of the woman's neck was gone, her bones and ligaments exposed. She had already taken on a gray pallor, and her veins had become dark beneath her flesh, standing out angrily.

Adam bent over the sink and splashed more water on his face. Suddenly something brushed against his foot. He looked down at the woman, who was beginning to moan and squirm. Curious, Adam thought.

Adam stopped what he was doing and focused on his victim. Who appeared to be going through a re-birth of some sort. Adam smiled as the woman flopped and struggled; it was amusing watching this beast come around. Something inside of him expected it, but he didn't know why.

The woman opened her eyes in full and looked up at Adam's grinning face. The boy reached his hand down toward the woman, who was now struggling to sit up. He grasped her hand in both of his own and pulled on the woman with all his might. A second later, the woman was sitting, her legs splayed open, and her dress bunched up around her waist.

"I'm hungry," the woman said in a deep, gravelly voice.

Growling, Adam replied, "Then feed yourself."

The woman groaned loudly. She was having a hard time controlling her body, and it didn't help that the closet was so small. An individual of that size needed room in which to get around. It was time for Adam to leave and give the woman all the room she needed.

"Thanks for the memories," Adam said with a sickening laugh. "Have fun, Fatty Patty." This comment brought a smile to the woman's face, even though it was offensive.

"Have fun, Fatty Patty," the woman echoed.

With that, Adam turned the door lever to the closet and opened it. He peeked out to see his father standing at the door of his cabin. His dad was holding a drink with a small plate on it. He quickly ducked back into the maintenance room and shut the door quietly. It wouldn't do for his father to see him. Not now, anyway.

The beast on the floor was gurgling as she fought to get to her feet. Adam kicked her hard and growled at her, motivating her to be still. He listened carefully to the sounds in the corridor, his ear plastered against the door.

"Adam, it's Daddy," his father's voice echoed. "I brought you some bacon and juice."

He heard him knock once again on the stateroom door, and then he heard the door rattle. He was going to go in, and he was okay with that. At least he wasn't in the room. His dad was beginning to sound and smell like an entrée to him. Since he had just eaten, it would be a waste to overindulge. He would bide his time with him. Besides, he had his heart set on sinking his teeth into that witch Claire. The thought got him all hungry and excited once again.

Adam then heard the door to the room open and close. All was quiet for a brief period, then the next sound he heard was the elevator bell, and moments after that, he listened to the elevator take off. He had left. It would be all clear for him to exit the closet.

He opened the door to the storage room and left the woman to fend for herself. After all, that's what he had to do, wasn't it? He made his way to the stateroom and locked the door behind him. As soon as he entered, he could detect the overpowering smell of bacon and juice, and both made him gag. He couldn't believe he had ever eaten this stuff before. Frustrated, Adam made his way to his parent's stateroom.

Adam then sat on their bed to rest, his eyes wide open and his breathing labored. He would just sit for a moment and watch his skin slough off as he waited for the perfect opportunity to come face to face with

Mother. Adam would like to have the woman for lunch, and he hoped that she had taken it lightly on the perfume. Fatty Patty's had nearly ruined his meal, but he had gotten past it.

So Adam sat on the bed and waited patiently for his next meal.

∞

Bruce was pleading with Doctor Anson for what seemed like hours. "Doctor, if unleashed this could start a disastrous chain reaction, a pandemic. You're a megalomaniac, you've gone too far."

"Bruce, calm down. This is what we have worked for all these years." Anson stated in a matter of fact tone.

"If you don't stop this madness, I have no choice but to notify the CDC and have you investigated," Bruce yelled with fury.

Anson saw red, and with fire in his eyes, he swung at Bruce with a mallet missing his head and striking him in the shoulder. Bruce picked up a chair and hit Anson, knocking him into the terrarium with the rat subject. Anson's hand flew into the terrarium, and instantly the varmint nipped at him, just barely breaking the skin.

Bruce acted fast, hitting the Doctor yet again, rendering him unconscious. "You're nothing but a mad scientist."

∞

Ariana lounged on a raft in the pool. She held her book up before her, as she listened to her favorite playlist that she had downloaded. Ari was so lost in her book and thinking about last night's party. That she had completely forgotten to check on Adam, she knew he wasn't feeling well and that her parents would be at the spa all day. She pushed the thought from her head as she recapped last night's events. The evening had been fantastic. The party was hopping, and the crew was so diverse there must have been one person from every country. She never met so many people at once, and from so many different countries. Ariana was having the time of her life on the cruise.

Claire was sitting in a chair, waiting for her massage appointment. "Did you check on Adam? How is he doing?" Jason had just walked in and joined her, taking note of three shopping bags his wife had obviously gotten from shops on the ship.

He sat next to her and said, "He wasn't in his cabin, so I left the bacon and juice. I assume he's feeling better if he's out and about." He took a deep breath. "What did you buy today, Claire?"

Her eyes lit up with excitement. "Oh, I found the most beautiful marble bookends at the gift shop, and I got Adam a leather case for his new phone, and for Ari, I picked a sweatshirt with a German Shepherd on the front. It also has the cutest little rhinestones, so I think she'll love it."

"I'm sure," Jason replied dryly. "As for Adam, I hope he's okay. It seems strange that he didn't touch base with us at all this morning. You would think he would come to one of us first thing and let us know how he is feeling, wouldn't you?"

"Well," Claire replied, "I'm sure he is dining somewhere, or maybe he has found his sister, and the two of them are in the pool. Who knows? I can tell you for sure that the boy won't come to me. It's you he prefers to deal with. I think we, as grownups, can admit that now can't we?"

Jason nodded and waved his hand with impatience. "I would think you would show a little more concern for our youngest child, being he is the one we have to worry the most about."

An African-American woman with long dreadlocks appeared. "Jason and Claire Harrington?" She was smiling brightly and seemed very friendly.

"That's us," Claire said as she stood. "Can I put my bags behind the counter, or in another safe place?"

The masseuse reached for the bags. "I'll take care of those for you," she said with a smile. "Now, if you'll just follow me, you are both in for a real treat!"

Jason looked at Claire and smiled. He could sure use a bit of serious relaxation right about now. He pushed his thoughts of his sick son out of his mind and followed the masseuse into the back.

Some spa time was just what both of them needed.

∞

Fatty Patty sat on the floor of the maintenance closet in a pool of her blood, which was rapidly congealing. Her neck was tingling severely, and she reached up to scratch at it with her hand. There was a gaping hole in her throat, and the fact was not registering well in her now-dead mind. It seemed she was functioning from the inside of a cloud.

She was simply dying of starvation, and only one thing appealed to her hunger: human flesh.

Patty put her hands on the floor and tried to push herself to her feet. She rose about half a foot, but when she tried to put her feet beneath her for support. They slipped in the gooey blood, and she came down hard on her butt. Patty growled in frustration, then tried again.

For a while, she looked like someone flopping around on wet ice, and it seemed she would never get to her feet. Then, just like that, she stood. She looked down at herself and began to laugh, which caused her to start choking. She got herself together and thought, I am a bloody klutz.

Unlike Adam, Patty did not see a point in cleaning herself up in the closet. Her husband was the captain of the ship, so nobody questioned her. She could make it to her quarters around the corner. There she would clean up, and then she would find her husband. He always had been the tastiest piece she had ever had. There was no reason to think he wouldn't satisfy her hunger today.

She left the closet and made her way to her large cabin. She saw no one, and it wouldn't have bothered her if she did. She was so relaxed that she hummed a tune as she lurched her way down the hall.

Her muscles seemed a bit stiff, but other than that and her ravenous hunger, she felt young again. It was time to sow a few of her wild oats. It was time to start enjoying the fact that she lived on a cruise ship.

It was time for Patty McElroy to have a little fun

CHAPTER 8

Bruce had Dr. Anson sedated in the exam room. He told the secretary Meredith Monroe that Anson's vehicle lost control and sent him off the road. The wreck wasn't huge, but Anson took a big enough hit to injure himself terribly.

So, Bruce recommended to keep him fully restrained and informed her of his exposure to lab animals, to take serious precautions. His scratch where the rat got him was looking infected, inflamed and had tissue necrosis. He could be contagious, and we can't send him to the hospital.

Dr. Anson was hooked up to machines and in a deep comatose state. Bruce thought he should try to get a hold of some of Anson's actual family. Anson's wife had divorced him when he announced his plans to take the study to Belize. Bruce left messages but received no callbacks; basically, Anson's wife told him no.

He intended to give it two more weeks. If Anson's condition had not changed any by then, he would unplug him. But for now, he was satisfied to wait. After all, things had significantly changed as far as the study was concerned.

Captain James McElroy left the control room after meeting with two of his men. He was ready for a spot of lunch, and he planned to meet his wife at the buffet. Now that the cruise was in full swing, he could begin to relax a little. The first few days were always the most demanding. Passengers had to settle in, and the crew had to get their flow going, but now everything seemed to be 'smooth sailing' for lack of a better term.

He rode the elevator and then made his way to the buffet, greeting everyone he passed with a nod and a smile. He was in an excellent mood. The day was beautiful and clear, and everyone seemed to be having the finest time. Captain McElroy was pleased.

"Hello, Esther," he greeted the buffet hostess. "How are things going today?"

The girl flashed him a million-dollar smile. "Excellent, sir," she replied. "Will you and the missus, have your usual table today?"

"Of course. Is Patty not here yet?"

Esther shook her head, the smile glued securely in place. "No, but I'm sure she'll be coming along shortly." She began walking the captain to the usual table and thought to herself, does it look to you like your wife misses meals much? The woman's weight was a running joke amongst the ship's crew.

As he sat, Esther asked, "The usual beverages, sir?"

"Yes, thank you," he answered. He always had a dark lager with his meal, and the missus drank red wine, a lot of it.

She left him to put in the beverage order, and the captain kept his eyes on the door. He looked at his watch; he had been a couple of minutes late, and usually, she beat him here by a mile. Today was certainly out of the ordinary. She knew he had to get back to work. He decided to fill a plate at the buffet and get started without her. She would get here soon enough.

Captain McElroy chose the sliced prime rib, a baked potato with the works, and a green salad. He figured that by the time he got back to the table, Patty would be there, but the only things that had arrived were the beverages. He put his plate down and looked around the room, thus far no Patty.

He sat down and began to eat, however he found he was getting antsy. The captain and his wife were creatures of habit, and they rarely deviated from their routine. He was becoming concerned. She hadn't contacted him to tell him she would be late. Where could she be?

He cleared his plate but decided against dessert. He had just enough time to get to his cabin to check on his wife, and that was what he chose to do. He downed his lager and walked back up to Esther.

"I'm not sure where Patty is," he began. "I am going to our stateroom to see if I can find her. If she comes in, will you let her know I'm sorry I missed her?"

With that dazzling smile again, Esther replied, "Absolutely, sir!"

With that, he made his way to the elevator. Perhaps she had taken ill and slept through calling him. That could be. He just needed to verify, so he didn't worry himself sick.

He rode the elevator, humming to himself as he did.

∞

Claire Harrington moaned at the touch of her masseuse. Her husband was on the table next to her. But that didn't keep her from giving off intense noises of pleasure. She thought that her sounds would rub in his lack of sexual attention, and the thought of his disgrace and embarrassment made her smile.

When they were finished, the two decided to have a late lunch.

"I'm going to go check on Adam," Jason said. "Maybe he'll want to join us. Will you see if Ariana is hungry? She should be at the pool."

Claire agreed, and the two went their separate ways. When Jason reached Adam's cabin, he hesitated. What was all over the floor at the end of the hall? He looked back at his son's cabin for only a moment, then pulled himself away and went to see the mess. He couldn't be sure, but from where he stood, it looked like blood and a lot of it.

He slowly approached and soon saw it clearly: yes, there was blood. It even looked like a bit of tissue! Jason gagged and took a few steps back. It looked as if someone had been murdered there! He looked around for someone, anyone, but the hall was deserted. Now he turned and jogged back to Adam's cabin. He entered the room, "Adam!" he shouted. "Adam, if you are in here, you need to let me know!"

There was no response, only silence, nothing. After another moment, Jason left the room and got back on the elevator. He needed to find one of the ship's staff and report all that blood.

Claire looked all over the deck for Ariana, but she was nowhere to be found. She probably wasn't even on the pool deck. Sometimes Jason could be such a slacker, especially when it came to the kids. She shook her head in outrage and took the stairs where she continued her search. No Ariana there either.

She would look in Ariana's cabin. If she didn't find her there, she was going to go to the bistro and meet her husband. If Ariana got hungry enough, she would find them, or she would get something to eat on her own. Daddy's little Sunshine was a woman now, after all.

Claire knocked on Ariana's door but got no answer. She shrugged her shoulders and rolled her eyes. Sometimes these kids pissed her off. She decided to stop into her cabin and grab a light jacket since she was here. The breeze from the water was giving her goosebumps.

She unlocked her suite door and walked inside. The jacket she wanted was draped across the back of a chair. She took off the wrap she was wearing and prepared to put the coat on. That was when she heard a noise in the bathroom.

Claire turned and stared at the bathroom door. "Jason?"

Now, something clattered to the floor in there.

"Jason, what are you doing? I'm starved." She walked over to it and turned the handle. Suddenly the door flew open, and before she knew what was happening, she was being jerked inside the bathroom violently.

A deep growl was all she heard, and then the arms were around her. The jacket slipped from her hands and hit the floor, and she began to struggle in full. Her attacker was powerful, and the more she fought, the weaker she got.

The bathroom lights were out, but the sunlight from the main cabin provided her with just enough light to see. It was Adam. He was covered in blood, he looked like something from a terrible nightmare, and the entire situation seemed surreal to her. Claire immediately went into shock and began screaming.

Without warning, Adam sank his teeth into her cheek. Claire screamed as loud as she could, her legs kicking and her arms flailing, but she was no match. Her mind could not wrap around what was going on.

"Don't worry, Mother," Adam gurgled as he held fast to her squirming body. "Soon enough, you'll have plenty to eat." He pulled her to him and bit down hard on her shoulder. She screamed in pain and surprise, sobs escaping her, and she began to fight in earnest, but she was no match for his strength.

She completely slipped out of reality as the teeth sank into her neck, Adam ripped the flesh from her throat and let her go, dropping her to the floor, alongside the jacket. He stood there, chewing on a large flap of her skin, and she watched him in shock as her hand went to her neck. Blood was pumping from the hole full force, and Claire knew with certainty that she was going to die. She was going to die at the hands of her twelve-year-old son!

He ripped more skin from her shoulder, then her arm. Claire watched him chew as blood ran down to her wrist and onto the floor. He stopped chomping suddenly and looked her in the eye. She was in utter and complete shock as she bled out on the cabin floor.

"Tasty," he said, then Adam lunged forward and bit deeply into her neck, for the second time completely severing her jugular. She immediately passed out.

Adam was dropping pieces of tissue to the floor from his mouth as he finished eating the mouthful he had just stolen from her. He then flipped on the bathroom light and sat down beside her to eat a bit more before she woke and joined him.

Claire's body twitched, and her arms were flailing around in unnatural positions, she appeared to be having a seizure. Then she stood up twitching and shaking as she made her way to her son, he stared at her with his mouth wide open chewing on muscle. He was moving his lips as if to speak, but no words were coming out, just wet smacking sounds. She knelt on the floor beside him, smiling, and lowered her mouth onto his eye socket. She bit down hard, popping the eyeball out immediately.

It was wonderful. It had a nice, firm texture and was full of flavor. Claire enjoyed it, savoring the taste of it with her eyes closed. Heavenly, simply heavenly!

Adam had stopped moving altogether now. He just lay on the bloody floor staring blankly out of his one eye. Claire indulged herself in another bite and then sat against the wall to chew it. She knew that shortly he would be waking up again, and she thought it was best if she was the first person her son saw when he came to. She wouldn't want him having to go it alone. After all, he was her son.

They couldn't wait for Daddy to come.

CHAPTER 9

The current batch of rats was violent, and they wouldn't die for good. Bruce knew the implications, but Dr. Anson had never created an antidote. If he had Bruce knew nothing of it. With his limited knowledge, he was winging it in regard to the studies they had been doing, and it terrified him. Bruce was only a petty assistant. He didn't have the knowledge or experience to rectify any wrongs. He didn't know how to stop what they had started.

The real problem, though, was in the fact that the current batch of rats ended up dying. But in only minutes, all of them came back to life. It had been very, very exciting.

The thing was, something was wrong with them.

They were violent, and became cannibalistic, eating each other. Every time one ate another, the mangled corpse would rise again. It didn't matter that the life form no longer had fur or skin. It didn't matter if they were missing limbs. The monsters came back anyway, and around and around it went, perpetuating over and over again.

Bruce sat at his desk in the lab, watching a rat that

had been murdered twice by the others. He was slowly but surely coming to again. Fear coursed through Bruce's veins and made his arms and legs tingle.

It was a good thing that Dr. Anson was restrained in the other room. Eventually, he would have started testing on larger animals, maybe even human subjects! Bruce was certain, and he was thankful that Anson was absent.

Bruce West was fully convinced that his mentor was nothing more than a madman. Yes, Bruce believed in their studies, but he didn't agree with Anson's theory that the studies should be completed at any cost. Anson thought that people dying for the cause would be acceptable, and that, in the end, was the reason they had to move the study to Belize.

Anson even had plans to begin testing on local vagrants once the serum began to show promise. He had been eyeballing every homeless person and drug addict he came across, but fortunately, he never had the opportunity to initiate those tests. Bruce couldn't help but be thankful for that fact.

Now the cycle was in full swing. Rats were eating each other, then dying, then coming back to life and starting all over again. He didn't know what to do, except keep them contained and allow it to go on.

But Anson was supposedly the only one who knew how to stop the cycle, and Bruce wasn't even sure that was true. He didn't think Anson expected success, and there was nothing in his notes or records that would help Bruce put a stop to it. Bruce had searched, time and again, over and over, having minimal benefit. He could do nothing, and the rats kept living and living and living.

∞

"I'm pretty sure someone had an accident or something," Jason was saying. He had found a single stewardess, and together they took the stairs back to the bloody corridor.

As they approached the mess, the woman sucked in air sharply. "Oh My!" she said. "I would say someone is badly hurt. I'm going to get in touch with the ship's doctor and the captain." She opened the door to the maintenance closet to fetch some wet floor signs to place around the blood. As soon as the door opened, she screamed.

Jason ran up to her. "What is it?"

She had her hand over her mouth and was shaking severely. Jason looked inside and sucked in a breath of his own. Blood was everywhere, and it looked as though someone had been splashing around in it.

Jason took the woman by the arm and pulled her away from the closet. "You go get the ship's doctor, and I will get the captain, okay?" She didn't answer him. She only stared at him with eyes as big as saucers and her hand over her mouth.

Jason gave her a shake. "Do you hear me? Go fetch the ship's doctor!"

She seemed to snap out of it then and ran to the elevator in her low, sensible heels. Jason was right on her tail. Something terrible had happened on the deck, and he wanted to make sure there wasn't someone dead in a cabin or a serial killer on board.

They went their separate ways off the elevator, and Jason saw a deck officer with a clipboard standing near the railing at the end of the corridor. He began to walk to him quickly and eventually broke into a jog. "Excuse me," he hollered, waving his arm. "You there! Excuse me!"

The deck officer looked up, startled by the man. He began to walk to Jason.

"How can I help you," he asked when they reached each other.

Jason stopped, panting. "There has been some kind of accident," he began as he caught his breath. "There is blood everywhere."

The deck officer, whose nametag read 'Oliver,' squinted at Jason as he tried to make sense of his words. "Who was hurt?"

"I don't know," Jason replied. "There is no one around, but the corridor is a bloody mess, and the maintenance closet looks as if someone was slaughtered in there."

He got his breathing calmed a bit and continued. "I took one of the stewardesses to see. She went to get the doctor, and I'm trying to find the captain. Can you tell me where to find him?"

"Come with me," Oliver said. "He should be in either the navigation room or his office." He glanced at his watch. "It's past his lunchtime, so I'm sure he is in one of those two places."

Oliver led Jason to the ship's bridge. The captain wasn't there, and he wasn't in his office either. None of the present crew knew where he was.

"I'll tell you what," the deck officer began. "Take me to the mess, and we'll go from there. If someone has been hurt, we need to find them. Hopefully, the stewardess you spoke with will have some luck. Maybe the individual has been seen by the doctor already."

∞

Ariana was talking with Brice in his office. They were having a great time laughing and giggling.

"I'm dog-sitting tonight, maybe after?" She offered.

Just then a stewardess barged in, "Doctor, I'm sorry, we need you."

Brice stood and looked at Ariana, "I'm sorry duty calls."

Brice followed the stewardess onto the elevator.

When Jason and Oliver arrived at the mess, the stewardess and ship's doctor were already there, and they were staring at all the blood with their mouths wide open.

"Have you treated anyone whose injuries could have made this mess," Oliver asked Brice.

He shook his head. "No one. Has the captain been notified?"

"We can't find him," said Jason.

The stewardess snapped out of her trance. "Should I have maintenance come and clean this up?"

"No!" said the doctor sternly. "We need to block off this corridor and let those residing in cabins here know that it will be off-limits for a while. I'll get the captain. Don't do anything until he sees it and makes his determination."

"My cabin is right down there," said Jason. "I'm just going to get my wife and kids, and then we'll hang out at one of the pools until you give the all-clear."

The doctor, stewardess, and deck officer boarded the elevator together, and Jason went to his cabin. He opened the door to see Claire sitting at the vanity with her back to him. Was she just sitting there primping?

"Claire, I just remembered Ariana is dog sitting for the Strickland's, she told us at breakfast. Why are you not at the bistro? There is a bloody mess in the hall, and we will all need to leave this level," he stared at the back of her head and tapped his foot in frustration. "I'm going to go get Adam."

"Adam isn't sick anymore," Claire stated, her voice light and airy as if she didn't have a care in the world.

Jason stared harder. She hadn't moved a muscle except for her mouth since he walked in. She just sat rigidly before the mirror.

"Claire, are you alright?"

She made a sound much like she was trying to clear her throat. Her response was low and guttural. "Wonderful, dear." With that, she reached up and turned the light to the vanity off. It had been the only light in the room, and the heavy curtains were closed. "I just want a little kiss, and then I will get the kids."

"Look, we really don't..."

"Please, Jason," Claire persisted. "Just one kiss."

He let out a ragged breath in frustration. "Fine, but we need to keep moving."

He approached her in the darkness and put both of his hands on her shoulders. Then Jason bent down to kiss her. Her lips came up and met his. The kiss was brief.

"You're freezing cold, Claire!" Jason said. "And your jacket is all wet. What the…"

Right then, she lunged upward at him and caught his lips in her mouth. She bit through them as if they were butter and tore the flesh from his face. Jason screamed and staggered backward, reaching out for the chair to steady himself.

The vanity light came back on then, and Claire turned to look at him. Jason's eyes grew wide. Her face was all chewed up, and her neck was ripped to shreds. He was stunned.

He was confused, and it felt like what was happening was a dream moving in slow motion. "Where are the kids?" His words had no annunciation, and they slurred terribly without his lips.

She stood and began to walk toward him, her body loping and jerking with the effort. "Adam already had his lunch," she said with half a smile. "I am ready for mine."

Jason reached his hand out to help steady her, staring at her mangled countenance. His wife took his hand and pulled herself to him, and like a flash, she sprang, making him topple over the back of the chair. She was on him then, biting and chewing, biting and chewing. Jason was in such shock he couldn't even scream. He tried to bat at her with his hands, but he was no match.

And the lights went out for Jason Harrington.

∞

Katy was in the middle of telling Emily and her Mother that the ceremony couldn't take place on the aft pool and that they would need to relocate. That's when Bridezilla went into a fit of rage!

"This isn't what I wanted, and you haven't done a single thing we've talked about. My Mom and I have been planning this for months! Now you're saying we can't even have the wedding where we expected due to a stupid clean up? How long does a damn cleanup take? This is ridiculous. You've single-handedly ruined what should be the best day of my life!" Emily exclaimed in an irate tone.

Maryann Rogers attempted to soothe her child, "it's okay sweetie, I'm sure they have put you in an equally amazing location on the ship. Your wedding is not ruined. We can still make this right." The fuming Bride began to calm with the sound of her Mom's soothing voice.

"But mom, I had every detailed planned, now it won't be what I imagined."

CHAPTER 10

Bruce stood with his coffee cup and made his way out of the lab. He needed a refill badly. He had to try and figure out how to stop all of this. There was something unnatural about it all. Something evil.

As he poured his coffee, he thought about the last batch of rats that had died before the big 'breakthrough.' The ones he tossed in the trash. They had injected them with the DNA-altering genome, as usual. Right away, two of the ten rats in the test died. But the other eight, the other eight had begun to change. First, their eyes went black, all of them. Next, patches of their fur had fallen out. At that point, four more died, and their deaths had been very graphic. When Bruce came into the lab the following day, he found the dead four with blood and mucus coming out of every orifice in their bodies.

Now there had been only four left, and the next stage of their 'transformation' consisted of veins that darkened under their skin, which had turned an unearthly shade of gray. Three more died that very night, leaving only one. That rat's eyes turned milky white, and he became violent. There was a mirror in their cage, and the rodent had run into it head-first and snarling until it had beat itself to death.

Bruce had disposed of all the dead rats in a knotted plastic bag right before a rainstorm hit, and when he took them out, he had taken notice of the dog. The same stray mutt that had been hanging out in the side alley for weeks. The dog, in and of itself, did not concern the lab assistant.

No, his concerns began only with the current batch of test rats, the ones that had survived.

The ones that were still surviving, even through death, over and over again.

He took his coffee and walked back to the lab, and the door open with a whisper. It was then that he heard the high-pitched screaming coming from the cage.

Bruce put his coffee on the desk and quickly walked over to the enclosure. There were still ten, but they no longer looked like rats. They had eaten at each other and died and then resurrected so many times that they resembled nothing more than balls of raw hamburger with milky-white eyes and sporadic tufts of fur. It was enough to make him want to puke his guts up.

Bruce was horrified, but the show must go on, according to Dr. Anson. Now Bruce knew that he should try to do something, anything, to put a stop to the madness. The problem remained that he simply did not know how to stop the nightmare they had started. Only Dr. Jonathan Anson knew that, and Jonathan Anson was not talking.

This cycle was something he knew would not end, at

least not on a positive note. Nothing that died over and over again and then came back to life could be 'positive.' His ulcer burned with concern, and his mind ached with wonder. He had already gone through all of Anson's files, and there was no remedy, no antidote, for what was going on.

To be honest, he was convinced at this point that Dr. Anson never believed his theories could be proved. The man seemed to be doing nothing more than playing games, playing God. Bruce West cleared his throat to keep from vomiting, took a deep breath, and went back to the computer at his desk.

He sat down and brought up his e-mail program. He then addressed his next e-mail to the CDC, Centers for Disease Control in the United States. He wrote the following:

To Whom It May Concern:

My name is Bruce West. I am a laboratory assistant to Dr. Jonathan Anson. He originally began experimenting with life-after-death sciences in the last few years, which, until the last six or eight months, had been funded by the United States Government. After our research was found to be detrimental, Dr. Anson moved the project here, to Belize, where the law would allow him to carry on experimentation that applied to his theories.

The reason for my letter is my great concern.

Dr. Anson's serums he had been testing began to take hold. While this may be terrific news to you, I must also inform you that it has resulted in an unstoppable life force, which I have no idea how to control. Dr. Anson left me no remedy to the issue. I believe that he did not think his research would be effective, and therefore a solution was omitted.

At the current time, our laboratory subjects have broken the boundaries of life and being unable to control the outcome. I am quite afraid of the consequences. I've taken it upon myself to bring this to the CDC's attention, without consent from Dr. Anson. Please contact me at your earliest convenience to discuss the situation.

Sincerely,
Bruce West, BioSearch

He made sure his main address, email, and telephone number were included in the information at the header. All he could do now was push send and wait, and wait he would.

∞

Captain McElroy was making his way to his cabin to find his wife when the ship's doctor caught up to him.

"Captain McElroy," the man began, his voice urgent. "It seems we have had an incident in one of the corridors. I need you to come with me, please."

"What kind of incident," the captain asked as he began to follow Brice to the elevator.

"I'm not sure," he replied. "There is a lot of blood all over the corridor and in the maintenance closet, but no one has come to me seeking treatment. Whoever bled that much is very likely dead, but there is no one there."

The two men reached the deck and got off the elevator. They began walking down the corridor toward the mess, but the captain saw it while they were still a reasonable distance away.

The captain walked up to the maintenance closet and opened it slightly, only to put his hand over his mouth and slam it shut again. "I would have to agree with you. Whoever bled this much should be dead."

Brice crossed his arms over his chest. "What should we do?"

"I'll have someone come clean this up," he began. "We can't have the passengers seeing this. Panic will break out."

McElroy got on his radio and called maintenance to the site, then turned his attention back to the doctor. "Get all the stewards and stewardesses together. We will need to go from room to room, one at a time, until we find out who this blood belongs to. If we have a dead body somewhere, we need to find it."

"I'll notify the deck officers and have them gather the stewards right away," Brice replied. He left the captain and got on the elevator to speak with the deck officers.

The captain just stood there, looking around. It was all he could do to shake his head in dismay. He hoped that no one was dead on board, but it sure as heck looked like there was.

He waited there until maintenance arrived, and he

proceeded to direct them to clean the mess up until it was spotless. He then waited for the deck officers and stewards to come, which they did expeditiously.

"I want you all to split up into three groups," he began. "Each group will take a level, and you will knock on every door there is. You will go into every room on board, every closet. Leave no stone unturned. Someone on this ship is either badly hurt or deceased. Find them. Don't mention anything to any of the passengers other than to ask if someone has been hurt. Understood?"

They all nodded in agreement, and many yes sirs echoed in his direction. With that, Captain McElroy made his way to his room. He had to find Patty and let her know what had happened.

He arrived at his quarters quickly and used his key card to enter the locked door. The room was well lit by the sunlight coming through the windows. He stood and looked around the room.

"Patty?" he shouted but was answered with silence. He shook his head and turned to leave. There was Patty, bloodied and ravaged, with a fire ax raised over her head. "What the heck are you doing?"

Patty smiled, and bubbles of blood came out of her mouth as she gurgled something he didn't understand. Suddenly the ax came down hard. Patty buried the blade right where his shoulder and neck met, and she buried it to the hilt.

James McElroy cried out and fell to the floor. Patty struggled clumsily to take the ax from his body but to no avail. It was stuck tight. She looked at all the blood out of one milky white eye and smiled. Then she bent down and began to dine on the captain's motionless body.

"Don't worry, dear," Patty gurgled between bites. "You'll feel like yourself soon enough."

∞

Adam and Claire had indulged themselves on Jason's flesh, then went their separate ways. Adam had wanted his father for himself, but Mom had gotten to him first, so he went to find his next meal elsewhere. No matter how much they ate, the hunger did not go away. It was a constant mission.

Adam had taken to walking the halls. He had a hoodie on, and the hood was pulled up to hide his face. It wouldn't do to scare off his supper.

Most of the passengers were enjoying the ship's amenities, though, and the corridors were pretty dead. That fact made it hard to find a meal, but it made eating a meal once you caught it very simple indeed.

He staggered up and down the corridors. Suddenly a cute girl about his age came around the corner. She saw him and said, "Hello!"

"Hello," Adam replied in a low, rough voice. He watched her as she struggled with her cabin door.

She turned to him and laughed, embarrassed. "The door hasn't worked well since we boarded. You have to jiggle it just right…"

"Let me help," Adam said, keeping his head low so she would not see his gaping eye socket.

She giggled once again. "Thanks." She then handed

him the key card and stepped back to give him room.

In seconds, Adam had the door open, and the girl stepped into her cabin. She turned around to thank him, and suddenly he tackled her. The girl flew backward into the room, landing on the floor. Her eyes closed against the pain of the wind being knocked out of her, then she opened them.

The boy on top of her was bloody and torn, and he was smiling at her through one eye.

CHAPTER 11

The cool brisk air blew the curtains open as Ariana shut the sliding glass door to the balcony. Her dog sitting adventure was going well. The couple would be back soon, and Ariana could care less, she would happily spend the rest of the cruise with the adorable Pomeranian, if given the opportunity. Suddenly there was a rustling at the suite door. Ari looked at Phu-fa-lou, "your mommy and daddy are here sweetie," she exclaimed in a soothing voice. The dog jumped to attention tail wagging in full force, rushing to the door, excitedly waiting for her owners to return.

Finally, the door creaked open, and the elderly couple fell into the room, staggering and growling with spittle dripping from their lips. Ari's heart sank as she saw the couple's monstrous state; with a pounding heart, she jumped and tried to reach for the poor puppy but was unsuccessful. The innocent creature was going crazy, barking and yapping, as the two owners knelt to their knees and attacked the dog.

Ariana was in shock, eyes wide with fear as she let out an ear-piercing scream, quickly she backed herself into the bathroom and latched the door shut. She was traumatized by the scene that played out before her very eyes, gasping for air and scared for her life. All she could think about was the poor innocent pup, the rage and anger welling up inside her. She opened the closet, franticly searching for a weapon. She was shaking the hanger rods in an attempt to free it for defense. Mentally exhausted, she crumpled to the ground.

Phu-fa-lou's eyes fluttered open with her newfound life force guiding the way. She was starved like never before. Ankle-biter has never been a more accurate description for the fluff ball of disaster that was ready to take on the world.

∞

Captain McElroy had come to rather quickly after Patty was done with him. His head ached slightly, but other than that, he felt like he was on top of the world. McElroy could eat a horse, but that wasn't what was appealing to his taste right then. He wanted blood, fresh blood, and lots of it.

The captain left his quarters and took a service corridor. It seemed he knew what he was doing without any awareness at all. He wanted to feed, and he wanted everyone else on the ship to join him. He felt a strange drive to sink his teeth into as many people on board the vessel as possible. Though in his logical mind, he didn't know why. What he did know was that he was headed to the bridge, where he intended to tear out the radio system.

He knew it was vital to cut off any potential contact with land. All people would want to do was kill him, and he didn't feel the need to die at all. What he did want to do was captain his ship in any manner he saw fit, and without hindrance.

He was about ten feet from the bridge door when it swung open. Captain McElroy stepped to the side and concealed himself in a small closet. He heard the voice of Brice Cummings and a woman. They were talking about someone being hurt in another corridor. Their conversation made him smile.

When they were gone, McElroy came out of hiding and approached the bridge entryway. He grasped the handle and opened the door, then stepped inside and closed it tightly.

"Hey, Captain," said Charlie Mason. He was one of the deck officers, and much to the captain's delight, he was the only one on the bridge.

Now he reached for the door once again, this time flipping the lock. 'Hello, Charlie," he garbled, his back to the young man. "All's well at sea; I take it?"

"Yes, yes," Charlie replied. "Nothing has changed since you went to lunch."

McElroy walked over to a metal box with a fire extinguisher and ax inside. Without a second thought, he put his fist through the glass and grabbed the ax out of it. Then he took a deep breath and turned around.

"What the heck…?" Charlie had stood up from his chair and had a look of confusion and panic on his face. He laughed nervously. "Is there a fire somewhere, Captain?"

With that, McElroy swung the ax in roundhouse

fashion and sank the blade directly into the radio. It went in like a hot knife in butter, but he had a much more difficult time pulling it out. Charlie jumped out of the way and continued to back up until his back was against the wall. He watched, horrified, as Captain McElroy pulled and yanked awkwardly on the handle of the ax. He was hollering and growling, with spittle flying from his mouth.

Charlie got his first real look at the captain as the man fought with that ax. He took note of the blood and the ragged wounds all over his neck and face. His skin was a deep gray and appeared splotchy. Both Charlie's mouth and eyes went wide, and his knees buckled. He slid down the wall in a crouching position, petrified over the man he saw before him.

Suddenly the ax yanked loose from the radio, sparks flying after it. McElroy drew back and swung the ax one more time, breaking the ship's AIS system nearly in two. Pieces of metal and plastic flew through the air.

This time the ax came out of the equipment much more easily. The radio was dead, of that the captain was sure. He was standing before the communication station admiring his handiwork when he heard a muffled sob.

McElroy turned sharply to his right. There on the floor trembling, eyes wide with fear, was Charlie. He had wet himself, and the front of his uniform was drenched. The captain smiled a half-grin and chuckled in a gravelly voice.

"I forgot you were here, Charlie."

Charlie began to sob louder as the captain dropped

the ax to the floor next to him. He began loping toward Charlie, who was holding his hands out before him as if to push McElroy away. His eyes were clenched shut, and tears were running down his cheeks.

"Don't worry, my boy," McElroy spat with gusto. "It will only hurt for a second."

With that, the captain was on him. Charlie kicked his feet and swung his arms around aimlessly, his eyes still firmly closed. "Stop!" he screamed over and over.

McElroy wasted no time with this one. He simply bit into his neck and pulled away, taking a mouthful of flesh with him. Part of Charlie's ripped jugular vein hung out of his mouth and rested on his chin.

That was the last thing Charlie saw, McElroy, sucking in the blood vessel like a wet noodle.

R.W.K. Clark

CHAPTER 12

Clarissa Thompson had been working with the Centers for Disease Control for ten years and long years they had been. In the beginning, she was on a team of investigators and spent her working hours investigating new reports of disease outbreaks all around the globe. Then, during one investigation, Clarissa contracted a mild form of Ebola, and as a result, she was hospitalized for three long months. When she returned to work, she was given permanent light duty because she was perpetually weak and tired.

She flipped on the light in her office and turned on the computer. As she waited for it to boot up, she unpacked her attaché case, organizing files on her desk in the order she would be working on them. She put her sack lunch in the small refrigerator, and she proceeded to brew a pot of coffee.

Another day, another dollar.

She sat down at her computer, finally, and began to go through her email. Most of it was correspondence regarding cases that were already under investigation, laboratory results, and requests for her signature. She had one-hundred and twenty emails in her inbox in all that morning, and she knew she would be focusing on them for the next several hours.

Clarissa busied herself with the emails as well as making phone calls when needed. At eleven-thirty, she glanced at the clock, almost time to eat. She would take care of one more email, then go to the bathroom, followed by a break for lunch. Man, people loved to slam her with these damn emails, and it disgusted her.

She opened the next email in the inbox. It was a correspondence from a laboratory assistant in Belize, named Bruce West. She scanned it with her eyes initially, but the contents of the letter demanded far more attention. Either this Bruce West was a crazy person, or he had gotten himself, and everybody else, in more trouble than he understood.

According to the email, he and Dr. Jonathan Anson were conducting a study on prolonging life or eradicating death. Far-fetched? Maybe, but from the sounds of it, they had crossed some boundaries that were never meant to be crossed. It sounded like they had succeeded to a certain degree.

She read and re-read the email over and over, making sure she understood what the man was getting at. Finally, she admitted there was no other way to interpret it, and she picked up the receiver to her desk phone.

"Ray, could you come to my office for a moment?" She was going to have her supervisor give it a read and find out what he wanted her to do.

In minutes he was next to her, reading the

correspondence over her shoulder. He shook his head, his expression dazed. "I don't know; it sounds like he is trying to blow the whistle. Should we take him seriously?" he asked.

"Yes, I think so. If Bruce West is full of baloney, we can always press false report charges."

"So you want me to call him?" she asked.

Ray nodded. "Yeah, call him. Assess the situation and let me know what you find out and what you decide to do."

"Got it," she replied, and Ray Ashton left her office.

Clarissa picked up her phone, once again, and began to dial the telephone number supplied to her by Bruce West in Belize.

∞

Ariana looked up at the grate above her. She couldn't just stay in the closet waiting to die, because essentially that was what she was doing.

She pulled the suitcase directly underneath the vent and put the first aid kit on it. Next, she climbed up and used a nail clipper to unscrew the bolts. She removed the grille and put it on the floor. Then she listened.

She listened to the couple in the suite. She could hear their wails and screams and groans coming through the bathroom door.

Ariana had enough of all of this.

With her arms, she pulled herself up, pull-up style, into the mouth of the duct. She was in excellent shape. Pulling herself into the air duct was easy.

Once she was up, she looked all around her. The

ducts were dark, but wherever there was a grate, a bit of light shone into the ventilation shaft. That was what she would have to use to help her get around in them.

She would have to be quiet. She knew she could accomplish that feat, but she also recognized those animals had a keen sense of smell, almost like starving dogs. Which she had witnessed by watching the Strickland's. How she wished she had known if there were more and where they were congregated so she could avoid those sections of the ship altogether.

Ari began to move forward slowly but surely. She wasn't going to stay in the closet, waiting to die like a trapped mouse. If she was going to die, she was going to do it fighting.

∞

"Dr. West, my name is Clarissa Thompson, and we have received your correspondence, but before we can take any steps to investigate the issue, we need to know a few things." The woman from the CDC had a high-pitched, nasally voice, and she gave off the impression of disinterest.

Bruce sat forward at his desk and pressed the telephone receiver closer to his face. "I'm not a doctor," he replied. "I am, or was, the lab assistant to Dr. Jonathan Anson. It was his project. However, I will tell you anything you need to know if I am able to, anyway."

Bruce found himself utterly grateful for email. Ten years ago, it would have taken weeks for them to get back to him, but not in this day and age. They had contacted him surprisingly fast, and now he sat on the phone, relieved that he had someone listening to him regarding the issue. Now he just had to get them to come and contain the problem.

The woman cleared her throat. "What was the original purpose of the studies you have been doing with Dr. Anson?"

"The doctor was doing extensive testing and study in regard to prolonging life, even to the point of completely eradicating death," he responded simply.

The woman was quiet. Finally, she sniffed and continued. "Obviously, something has gone wrong, as per your correspondence. I will need more details, please."

Bruce knit his brow as he considered his words carefully. He didn't want these people to think he was some kind of wing-nut. He wanted them to clearly understand his concerns, mainly his worry about humans being cross-contaminated. If even one rat were to escape, the consequences would likely be irreversible.

"Dr. Anson has been working on developing a serum that would prolong life greatly, at the very least," he began. "At most, it would eradicate death."

"We were working on the study in the states for three and a half years, but then some of your investigators shut us down. They said we could not use animals of any kind to do the type of testing the study required. At least, not in the United States, that is." Bruce stopped and coughed into his hand, then continued. "So, we brought our study here to Belize."

"With that being said, what are you concerned

about?" the woman asked.

"The rats," he said. "They won't die, and they're very violent. They kill each other and even begin to eat the corpse, but within only minutes, they resurrect, and the cycle continues."

"Wait a minute, now," the woman said sharply. "You are telling me you have half-eaten rats that are coming back to life and continuing to kill and eat each other, only to come back to life again?" She sounded incredulous.

He cleared his throat. "Yes, ma'am, that is exactly what I am telling you. If one of them were to get out and say, bite a human or another animal, I don't think the issue could be put right if you know what I mean. This is why I went over his head to alert you."

"Did Dr. Anson neglect to provide some type of remedy or antidote if the study were to go awry?" The woman's voice was reaching a slightly alarming pitch.

"Yes, you're correct there is no antidote."

The phone was silent for a brief moment, then she said, "I will fill out a full report immediately and make sure a team gets it. It is out of our jurisdiction, but it has a reason for concern; they will get in touch with the governmental parties and make arrangements."

"Fine," Bruce said. "If you need to get in touch with me, you have my information. Thank you."

He hung up the phone and sat back in his chair. He watched the mangled rats feast on some part of a dead one. It was beginning to twitch to life, even as they dined.

All he could do was wait.

∞

Meredith was finishing up her shift at the BioSearch testing facility. She moved here five years ago from the states, and she had settled in quite nicely. She loved her job and loved Belize.

Meredith had only a couple of tasks left to check on, and then she could catch up on her charting. She was anxious to go home. She had a hot date with a Brazilian dancer, and he was nothing less than delicious.

She checked in on Bruce and picked up all the notes he had for her to chart. She then left the room and made her way to Dr. Anson.

Anson was restrained, heavily sedated, and his room was quarantined, the prognosis wasn't good. What a shame, he looked awful and the odor in the room was rancid.

Meredith busied herself with checking his vitals and making sure everything was hooked up correctly. She made sure the straps, securing Anson to the gurney, were all tight. They all looked fine, and she grabbed his chart from the foot of the bed to update it, humming as she did so—almost time to go.

"It's… It's too late, you know."

Meredith looked up; it was the doctor! He had just spoken! "Dr. Anson, it's Meredith, how do you feel? It's too late for what?" She leaned her head down so she could make out his words better.

"They won't die… they will never die," Anson gasped for breath.

Her heart was pounding. "It's okay, Dr. Anson. You're at the lab, and we are taking good care of you."

His eyelids fluttered, and life left him for good, the machine alarms beeping.

But it was too late for Dr. Jonathan Anson.

"Bruce, I was standing right here when Dr. Anson coded." Meredith was saying as the two of them worked over Anson for the next few minutes. She continued to fill him in on all the details of his previous and current condition. He was pronounced dead at 6:45 pm, and at 7:13 pm, he began to struggle violently.

"Luckily, we had him restrained," Meredith said.

"We will keep him restrained and heavily sedated for the time being until we can assess what exactly happened." Bruce's voice was tinged with terror. "I'm going back to the lab, could you please finish the charting before you leave?"

"Sure," she replied.

Bruce returned to his desk, and after a moment, he stood up and walked over to the containment cage. The rats that were dining had suddenly turned their attention away from eating and were congregating in one corner. It was as good an opportunity as any to take one of them and see where the chemical levels were. Since they had begun this macabre cycle, he hadn't done it. He was scared to death, but his curiosity and fear motivated him.

He put a pair of rubber gloves on, the industrial-strength kind, like the ones his mother had used to do the dishes when he was a boy. He opened the top of the cage and reached for the injured rat. It was still having spasms, and now sickening wet sounds were coming from its throat. He lifted it out of the cage quickly and let the lid slam shut.

The thing began to squirm in his hand almost immediately, but he kept a firm grip on it. He took it over to his station and laid it on the work table. Then he prepared a butterfly needle to take a blood sample. He turned back to the rat with the needle in his hand.

Right then, the rat seemed to take flight off the table. It landed on Bruce's shoulder and sank its teeth into his flesh through his white button-down shirt, then it pulled back, tearing a large chunk of tendon and cotton material. Bruce screamed and began hitting and slapping at his shoulder. The rat flew to the floor where it lay twitching and chewing, the cloth hanging from its mouth.

He ran to it and stomped on it as hard as he could. It was nothing more than a splatter on the floor when he was done, but it was still twitching. He stared at it, horrified. That's when he heard a noise behind him that he couldn't quite place. He turned his head to see the other rats in that cage, piling one on top of another. The rat on top of the heap opened the cage and was already on its way to Bruce. The noise he heard had been the cage door being flung open and hitting the wall behind it.

Bruce's mouth hung open in shock, and his eyes were wild with disbelief as he watched one rat after another lob themselves up and out of the cage. He tried to scream, but nothing would come out. He began to back away from the cage slowly, keeping his eye firmly on the little monsters. He had to get out of that lab.

He was just getting ready to turn around and run full force for the door when his knees hit the back of the stool at his workstation. He fell over it and landed hard on the floor on his back. The wind completely knocked out of him. As he gasped for breath, he watched the mutant rats head in his direction like a line of soldiers advancing for battle.

He could not breathe much less right himself from his position on the floor. In only seconds, they were on him, all over him, and they were beginning to feast. He couldn't scream, but he tried. The last thing he would be aware of was a rat biting into his Adam's apple. Then everything went black.

The CDC was in for a big surprise.

CHAPTER 13

It was the fourth day of the cruise, and most of the passengers were no longer themselves. Out of three-thousand individuals, there were only a few hundred that were still human, and all of them had gone into hiding. As for the crew, they had all changed but for a small handful, which included Brice Cummins, the ship's physician, and four others. One was Rick Harris, the ship's purser, Kevin Hines, a deck officer, a stewardess named Katy Richards, and George Meade, the chief officer who had been the captain's right-hand until he had turned bad.

The undead were taking over the ship. Passengers were in hiding, having barricaded themselves in cabins and other areas throughout the vessel in an effort to save themselves. Four of the five crew members were holed up on the bridge, and they were unable to call for help because the captain himself had destroyed the radio the day before. The only reason they had gotten access to the bridge once again was because he had left to find a bite to eat.

The hiding really didn't help much. The monsters seemed to be able to smell better than bloodhounds, and if they even got the smallest whiff of the living, they would become determined to have them.

They were being picked off, slowly but surely, and hope was nowhere to be found.

Ron Rogers, his wife and kids, and approximately twenty other passengers were hiding in the ship's fitness area. They had moved weight benches and treadmills up against the entrances to keep the cannibals out. The entire front of the fitness area was glass, and the skin eating souls were all around, looking in at the fresh meat and pounding and clawing at the glass with their fists. The captain and his wife were among them.

"It seems to be keeping them out," Ron said to the others. "I'm pretty sure they can't break through that glass; it's security glass after all."

Another man named Tom, said, "We can only hope. Does anyone know what the heck is going on?"

"No," Ron said simply. "All any of us know is that these flesh feeders want to eat us. You know as much as we do."

One of the zombies had picked up a cushioned chair that had been positioned by the outer main deck and was hitting the glass with very little benefit. The walking cadavers were getting angry and restless. Even their screams and growls were getting louder.

"They're getting worked up pretty good now," Ron continued. "I want all the women and children to get in the large back office area. Shut the doors and lock them." The women began to stand up and gather their children. They were more than willing.

Tom's voice was a bit panicky. "Why don't we just kill them? There has to be a way."

Ron turned to him as the last of the women and children disappeared to the back. "Before we all got together in here, I fought one, and I did damage that would have killed a normal man; I smashed his face in with a fire extinguisher! He just kept coming."

More zombies began to gather at the glass front, and they were becoming excessively agitated. Ron continued, "At one point, I had him on the floor, and I was hitting him in the head with it over and over. I thought he was dead, but as I backed away, he stood back up. I had to smash its head flat completely. I don't think the monsters can be killed any other way."

Tom's eyes were filled with terror. "We have to think of something. I don't wanna die on this damn ship!"

All of the men in the group sat there watching the rotters try to break their way through the glass.

"Yes," Ron said. "We have to figure something out, alright, or we're all destined to join them. Think everybody. We're in the middle of the damn ocean, keep that in mind."

∞

Ariana was crawling aimlessly through the ventilation shaft franticly trying to find her way in the darkness. She thought to herself; I have to find my family. The Strickland's suite couldn't be that far from her parents; Ariana was sure of it. If only she could find her way, she desperately needed her dad. As she came across another vent, she peered inside, looking for a hint of something familiar. That's when Ariana noticed her mother's enormous makeup bag. She let out a sigh of relief.

Ariana took the nail clipper from her pocket and worked on the screws securing the grille in place. Within moments she was lowering herself onto the vanity. When she saw the mess on the bathroom floor, it instantly took her breath away.

Without warning, a voice startled her, and she quickly turned around. "Ari we miss you honey, let me take your pain away!" Screeched her mother as she approached Ariana.

Ari was frantic, seeing her awful mother transformed into an even worse monster. It was time for the young, frightened girl to become a woman, a woman capable of defending herself. With determination and focus, Ariana stood tall in front of the woman that made her feel insignificant her entire life. "I'm sorry, mom," Ari said as she plunged a blunt nail file between the eyes of her dear wretched rotting mother. The woman's body fell to the floor with a thump, Ari watched the entire nightmare unfold before her very eyes.

When the limbs twitched for the final time, Ariana stepped around her mother's body and looked into the stateroom; she was met with silence. It was dark and quiet. The light was peeking through the heavy curtain. She thought to herself for a moment, contemplating whether or not to run for a lifeboat. She let out a breath and grasped the nail file tightly, looking at the weapon in her hand.

After a moment, Ariana slowly opened the cabin door and peeked into the hallway. There she saw a flesh-eater wandering aimlessly. As quiet as a mouse, she snuck out and approached the animated corpse from behind. It was looking around, sniffing the air. When suddenly it turned in her direction, it had obviously picked up her scent. Without missing a beat, Ariana plunged the nail file between its eyes, and it entered the side of the nasal bone. She continued to bury it to the hilt. Its body fell against the hallway wall and slid down, causing excessive noise. Alerting the horde around the corner, they all turned in the direction of the sound. Like a pack of rabid dogs, they came around the corner mouths frothing and headed straight for Ariana. She kicked the first one down, in roundhouse fashion, then stepped on its back to spike the next. As the nail file entered the second rotter it snapped in two, leaving her utterly defenseless. She turned on her heels and jumped from the struggling to rise cadaver. Its body was obstructing the hallway while attempting to stand, slowing down the rest of the pack. She headed as fast as she could back to the suite. Once inside, she flipped the deadbolt and made her way back into the ducts.

The scene was playing out in her mind over and over. She was proud of herself, and her confidence was growing quickly now. Yet, she felt this ping of remorse. While she knew she did what she had to, to survive, she couldn't help feeling guilt over ending her own mother's life. She desperately wanted to find Brice, and they would escape this horrid nightmare together. They would leave the ship in the middle of the ocean and, with luck, find a deserted island where they would live happily ever after. Was she delusional? An island, really? Her mind was swimming. She needed rest soon.

Ari continued crawling for what seemed like hours, and her eyes were heavy. It was pitch black. The air was blowing cold through the duct, keeping her comfortable. She came to another junction and decided to turn left. After crawling a bit, she noticed the change in the air. There was no breeze. It was musty, and the air was thick. This duct must lead nowhere, she thought to herself. Would this be a good place to rest? Exhaustion fell over her as she turned around and backtracked a few feet to find just enough air to relax. Finally, she felt safe for the time being.

∞

Clarissa Thompson hung up the phone from her conversation with Bruce West and sat back in her chair, thinking hard. Yes, his story sounded like a bunch of trumped-up hogwash. Yes, she was having a hard time believing him, but something inside her told her not to blow this off.

While she would never consider sending a team to Belize years ago, things were much different now. There was so much the human race had learned, so many advances in technology that she knew it might very well be possible to do the things that Bruce West said they were doing.

She was obligated to have it checked out.

She rang Ray at his desk. "I've spoken to the lab assistant in Belize," she told him. "In my opinion, we should send someone, and probably as soon as possible, just to be safe. Do you have preferences as to who we should send?"

Ray was quiet for a moment as he gave it some thought. Finally, he said, "First, let's get Carl Morgan there asap to initiate the investigation. If this is a legitimate claim, then send David Umbridge immediately. He is our expert. This could be a good case to let some of the newbies cut their teeth on. For additional assistance, send Kim Johnson and Keith Mitchell as well. They need the experience, but I want them with someone who knows what they are doing like Umbridge."

Clarissa was writing as quickly as he was talking. She would have to fill out the assignment orders for each individual, take care of booking flights for them, and make sure they were up to code on foreign procedures.

She hung up the phone and got four assignment order forms from her file cabinet. As she filled them out, she had a chill go down her spine. Something told her that this was not going to turn out to be an ordinary case. Something about the whole thing made her turn cold with concern. Maybe Ray was wrong; perhaps it wasn't such a good idea to include a couple of rookie team members on this assignment.

On the other hand, they could get down there and

discover that this Bruce West character was a raving psychopath who had recently escaped from some mental asylum. Clarissa smiled and shook her head at her thoughts. Ray knew the recruits better than they knew themselves. She would trust his judgment.

She pushed the thoughts from her mind and set about getting the team ready to go to Belize.

∞

Brice knew something no one else had come to realize. Everyone knew these were animals, the undead, and they were starving. Yes, they lurched around and struggled to make way in their dead bodies, and their appearance made them seem almost stupid. But Brice knew there was nothing stupid about them.

The way things had gone since this whole nightmare began seemed almost orchestrated. Brice chuckled to himself. It sounded ridiculous, but there was no mistaking it: these monsters were acting with intent. Sure, it was beyond their control, this taste for flesh, but they were advancing like troops in an army. Brice believed they intended to do the same thing on land.

Whatever had happened to these people, couldn't be allowed to reach land, but Brice was pretty sure he was going to have no say over that in the end. As far as he knew, this ship was the only place on Earth where this life-after-death thing seemed to be happening. If only they could keep the ship from docking. If only he had a way to warn people on land. But Brice could think of nothing but saving Ariana ultimately. He shook his thoughts of powerlessness out of his mind and reset his focus on the situation at hand.

He had hidden in one of the airflow ducts while searching for Ariana when he had come upon the captain. He was bent over a female figure in one of the corridors and was devouring her belly. Brice had crawled around through the ducts until he was able to see the captain clearly through one of the grates. What he witnessed shortly thereafter had enlightened him greatly.

Three zombies had come around the corner and into the corridor where the captain was having his grotesque meal. He had looked up at them and offered them a bloody smile. Suddenly he had stopped eating and stood up awkwardly.

"The ship is almost ours," he said simply to them. They replied with grunts and groans. "Keep up the good work. Soon we will take our new life to land."

With horror, Brice realized that his greatest fears were being played out right before his eyes. Not only were the dead people organized, but they also had a leader in Captain McElroy. This was very bad for everyone who may still be alive.

Brice worked his way through the ducts until he got to the bridge. He wanted to use the radio to call for help. When Brice reached the bridge, he was met by the other four crew members, who had already barricaded themselves in. He had never been so happy to see anyone in his life.

Kevin Hines, the deck officer, had unscrewed the grate from the roof so the doctor could join them.

"They are soldiering," he told them as he tried to clear his head.

"What do you mean, 'soldiering'?" Kevin's eyes were as wide as saucers.

Brice took turns looking at each of the others directly in the eyes. "The captain, he is sending them out like advancing soldiers. They intend to take over the entire ship and then dock. They are going to continue on land."

"What are we going to do?" Katy asked, her voice bordering on hysterical.

Brice turned to her. "First of all, keep calm. I'm going to radio land for help."

"Do you think we haven't thought of that?" This came from George, the chief officer. "Wow, really? Man, we aren't mentally deficient! The captain destroyed all the radio's wiring. There is no way to call for help. Not from the bridge anyway." George stated in a matter of fact tone.

Brice walked over to the radio to get a look. Sure enough, it was nothing more than a gaping hole with shredded wires coming out of it. On the floor beneath was the front panel and radio unit, shattered to bits.

"I guess he thought of everything," Brice said. The captain didn't want them to be able to contact land at all. He intentionally had taken the necessary steps to limit their ability to communicate.

He fully intended for everyone on board to die.

George spoke again. "You mean to tell me that these things are plotting to take over the ship? You mean to tell me they have any presence of mind at all?"

"Exactly, that's what I'm telling you."

All of them stood there on the bridge, looking defeated. Finally, Brice said, "We don't have a choice, people. We either have to figure out a way to kill them or a plan to get off this ship. We have no idea how many normal passengers there are, if any. We have to beat them, or we'll end up joining them." Brice continued, "please help me back into the air duct. I'm searching for someone."

"I wish you would reconsider," George said.

Brice ignored him. He had the grate off and was busy putting the pliers back in his pocket the best he could. "Help me up here, man," he said to George.

George just shook his head and gave Brice the boost he needed to get up into the air ducts. "Since you are staying, make sure you replace the grille. I'm sure you want to be as safe as you can for as long as possible."

"Yep. Already thought of that," George replied. He picked up the grate and the screws, then gave Kevin a look to help.

"Good luck, Brice."

"Thanks," he said. "I'm sure I'll need it."

R.W.K. Clark

CHAPTER 14

Captain McElroy stood on the massive deck. Before him, his new family was gathered. So many were there that they were trickling down the side corridors. It was a mass of monsters, grunting and howling.

"We have come a long way," he said through a bullhorn, which he held awkwardly in both hands.

He continued in a garbled voice, "Soon, we will be able to go to land and enjoy even bigger feasts than before."

The grunts and growls grew louder with approval.

"We must have everyone," the captain continued. "Leave no stone unturned. Treat yourselves to the delight of the victims, and know they will all be like us, even onto land."

The mob groaned with delight.

"Now, go!"

They began to disperse, some individually and others in groups slowly. Those who had been crowding around the fitness area returned there. Others began checking out the boutiques, bistros, and other businesses. They all went from cabin to cabin, business to business, leaving no stone unturned, just as the captain had demanded.

But the captain himself made his way to the bridge. He tried the handle on the entrance. It turned easily enough, but he couldn't get it to open. He could smell the fresh meat inside, and he knew he had to get in. He began to pound and kick at the door violently.

"I know you are in there," his garbled voice screamed.

He pressed his ear to the door and listened. Yes, he could hear them inside. A woman was crying hysterically, and someone was trying to speak soothingly to calm her down.

Now he began to get angry. He started beating on the door once again. Then he lurched off to find someone to help him. He wanted the people on the other side of that door.

Captain McElroy returned with five others, and together they began to throw themselves up against the door, some clawing at it as they did so.

"We will have you!" the captain shouted. He pressed his face against the door then began to run his tongue up and down on the surface. "We will have you…" He began to laugh hysterically, as did the others around him. It really was only a matter of time.

∞

Maryann's husband, Ron Rogers, sat on the floor of the fitness area with his knees bent and his back against the wall. His head was turned up toward the ceiling, and his eyes were closed. All he could do was turn things over and over in his mind. They had to figure out a way to kill these monsters, or they had to find a way off the ship.

After a moment, he stood and stretched. He turned to Tom and the other men. "I'm going to go check on the women and children."

He made his way to the back area, where the others were holed up. He quietly knocked on the door. "Maryann, it's me Ron, let me in." The door slowly opened allowing him to peek in on them. They were all huddled together, with many of the children sleeping soundly. A couple of women were crying, but they were keeping it down quite well. No one wanted to wake the kids up for any reason.

When he got back to the main fitness area, Karen's husband Tom was standing and pacing back and forth. He saw Ron and eagerly asked, "What about fire?"

"Fire?" Ron echoed.

Tom nodded. "Yes, fire. Maybe we could think of a way to set the ship on fire. If we could get to lifeboats, we could still get to land while these so-and-so burn."

Ron sat down on a weight bench, his back to the chaotic and violent zombies that were gathered at the security glass. "Fire. I don't see why it wouldn't work, but how would we get to the lifeboats without becoming victims ourselves. How would we start a fire that would be big enough to deal with these problems?"

The men all fell silent again as they pondered the suggestion. One of the men spoke up finally. "You know, we are sitting here watching these monsters trying to get in here at us, and you guys are talking about getting to the lifeboats safely? You're talking about lighting a fire? Do you realize the ship is all iron and steel?" Jay, the yoga instructor, spoke up with a sarcastic smirk and a whiney tone.

"You're right," Ron agreed as he thought to himself geez this guy is such a crybaby. "But we have to do something or die trying. These things are killing and eating people, and people are coming back to life and joining them. There is likely no way to do what you're suggesting, Tom."

"Well, why don't we at least look around and try to find an alternative way out of here," Tom continued. "Then, we could light the fire in here and escape from the area, letting it burn."

Ron thought about this. "There is no 'alternate' way out. There is only one exit."

Tom began to pace once again. "Well," he said in a frustrated voice. "We could at least look around. Maybe there is a trap door or even a fire exit we are not aware of."

"Fine," Ron replied. "Let's all go through this place thoroughly. Look for an emergency exit."

The men began looking all around the fitness center. There were two offices, one in which the women and children were hiding in, a restroom, and the storage area. They moved desks and boxes so they could see what was behind them. Ron had pretty much given up and returned to the main area, where two of the other three were waiting.

"Any luck?" he asked them.

A red-haired man shook his head and replied, "Nothing. Not even so much as a hatch in the floor."

Just then, they heard Tom's voice yelling. "Hey, guys. Come here!"

They found Tom in the storage room. They had all been in here; what could he have found that they missed?

"Look," he said with excitement. "Air duct. The grate is big. I'm sure we could easily fit inside."

Ron's wheels were turning. "And we would pretty much have access all around the ship. Good job, Tom."

"So, how should we handle this?" asked Tom.

Ron's eyes were fastened on the vent as he paced back and forth before it. "As of now, we have no way to start a fire, but if one of us went into the ducts, we would be able to do a couple of things."

"And?" asked the red-haired man.

"First, we could look for a way to start a fire. You know, matches, a lighter, or maybe some emergency flares. Second, we would be able to determine a safe passage from here to the lifeboats."

"So, who wants to go?" Tom asked.

"I will," Ron said immediately. He turned a trash can upside down and stood on it to get a closer look at the grate. "I am going to need something to remove these screws with."

The red-haired man snapped to attention. "I have a multi-purpose utility knife!" He dug his hand into the front pocket of his trousers and withdrew the tool.

Ron smiled. "Perfect, thanks Red!" He took the tool

from the man, and within five minutes, the grate was in his hands. He handed it down to Tom.

"Okay. I'm going to go and see what our options are. If I'm not back in an hour, you can assume the worst," Ron said. "Otherwise, I'll be back."

Ron was able to hoist himself up and into the duct with the help of the other men, and soon he was crawling on his hands and knees. Ron figured he could stop at any other vent and get a good idea where he was on the ship, and he would also be able to see just what the monsters were up to without giving himself away.

He got moving faster; there wasn't time to waste.

∞

Maryann Rogers sat on the floor of the fitness center's office area. She was holding her two youngest children, tightly to her bosom. There were three other women with her, and a total of seven kids, besides hers.

All the men had made her, along with the other women and children hide back here. They had locked the doors and piled up boxes of supplies against it. The ship was full of monsters. The beasts wanted to eat their flesh. It felt to Maryann as if her sanity were hanging on by a thread. It all seemed so unreal.

"Maryann, do you think they will find us back here?" A woman named Carol was asking the question. Maryann looked at her. She appeared to be on the edge of sanity herself.

"No, Carol," she replied, not believing herself at all. "I think we are safer than anyone else on this ship."

Carol breathed an audible sigh of relief and leaned

her head back against the wall and closed her eyes. "I just want to go to sleep and wake up when this is all over," she said.

"I know how you feel, Carol, but we have to worry about the kids." This was a woman named Karen speaking. She was married to the guy named Tom that was out in the central area with Maryann's husband, Ron.

"Yes," Maryann agreed. "We can't be letting our fear get the best of us. We can't panic. We have to think about the children."

She looked down at her kids, who had fallen into fitful periods of sleep. She was relieved. The less they knew or understood about what was going on, the better. She adjusted herself because her legs were going to sleep, then she settled back against the wall.

All they could do was sit in the storage area and wait. Maryann just knew there was nothing else they could do. The only problem was that she recognized that their backs were against the wall. She wasn't a stupid woman. It couldn't be good that they were locked in here; there was no place for any of them to run if they had to. They were all like fish in a barrel, just waiting to be shot.

She ran her fingers through her daughter Carly's sandy brown curls. The child's head was on her lap, and she was sleeping peacefully. Oh, to be a child again! Oblivious to everything around them. Unaware of the nasty reality of life and grown-up problems.

Now Maryann looked down at the face of her son,

Curt. He was eight and wanted terribly to be a grown man already. She smiled to herself with amusement. He had the longest eyelashes. She wondered how they didn't tangle together as he slept.

She knew deep in her heart that no one in that room was ever going to walk off that ship, at least, not in the same state as they walked on to it. She knew every last one of them was going to die, and more than likely, they would all end up walking corpses, just like the monsters that wanted so badly to eat them.

Maryann closed her eyes and tilted her head back against the wall. Why did her oldest insist on a wedding on this stupid cruise? She had wanted her to have a local wedding, but Ron thought the wedding party would enjoy spending a week in the middle of the ocean. He had been right; when they gave the kids a choice, she had been outvoted.

She should have put her foot down, had a fit, or something. In retrospect, she could think of a thousand things she could have done, and it made her shake with frustration that she hadn't done any of them. She had a bad feeling from the start, and now there was nothing she could do to fix the mess.

Carly stirred a bit, breaking her mother's thought process. Maryann let the girl twist and turn as she repositioned herself, then she was sleeping again. Maryann closed her eyes once again and tried to shut out her reality long enough to get a little sleep.

CHAPTER 15

Carl Morgan had been with the CDC for a few years now. He figured he would go to the site, check it out, and be able to give the all-clear to HQ. He had been assigned to initiate this investigation, and if further help was needed, he would send for three others that were on standby. From the sounds of it, the person who reported this was off his bloody rocker. He didn't think the others would have to bother with the mess at all. This sounded like a wild goose chase, trumped up by a raving lunatic. It wouldn't be his first rodeo. Wackjobs seem to enjoy making false reports and wasting his time.

"This is the street," he said to himself as he took a left turn. He kept his eyes on the building, looking for the telltale numbers that would let him know he had arrived. He drove a full five minutes before he found the place, a brick building situated on a filthy alleyway with no significant signs or markings that would give away what was done there.

He pulled up in front of it and got out of the car. Then he fetched his case of equipment out of the trunk, and after making sure that the vehicle was securely locked, he began to advance toward the building.

First, he looked down the alley. It was apparent that this is where the garbage was taken. He would take a look there after he talked to this Bruce West character and examined the rats he was concerned about. Carl made a mental note and then went up the short set of concrete steps that led to the building's main entrance.

The door opened effortlessly, and he stepped inside. There was a desk with a telephone, but no secretary. At the far end of the entryway, there was a single door with a red and white sign that read 'Restricted.'

Without hesitation, he went to the door and opened it, peeking his head inside. There was a corridor with several doors, and all of them were closed. Each had a small square window in it, and he decided he would peek inside each.

"Mr. West?" he hollered as he went from door to door. "Mr. West, it's Carl Morgan with the CDC. I'm here to investigate your report." Carl repeated as he listened while looking around, he was met with nothing but silence and musty stale air.

He stopped at each door in the corridor and carefully listened after he looked through the window. He thought he could hear noises coming from behind one of the doors at the end of the hall, but they didn't sound human. He made his way down there, stopping at a few of the entries and looking through the little glass windows. He saw what appeared to be exam rooms, some offices with empty desks, and filing cabinets. Only two of the offices seemed to be in use.

He trudged on and came to the last door. The

sounds coming from it were louder now. Carl looked through the glass and caught his breath.

Two people were lying on the floor. One was a woman with blood-matted hair. She appeared to be trying to sit up, but she couldn't get her footing at all. She looked like a fish out of the water. It seemed like she didn't know how to walk in the high-heels she was wearing, as if it were her first time. If she hadn't been a bloody mess, Carl Morgan would have been amused by the scene before him.

A man was lying next to her. He appeared to be alive, even though he was hardly recognizable as being human. He looked to be all chewed up. He was flailing his arms in an effort to get what looked like mutated animals off of him, but he wasn't having much luck. The animals, or whatever they were, obviously had the upper hand in the situation.

Carl stepped back away from the door quickly, his heart pounding and his forehead dripping sweat. What the heck was all that about? The report he had been given signified that scientific studies were being done here, which had to do with prolonging human life or eradicating death. Obviously, they had been using rats, and things had gone awry.

But he had not been adequately prepared in his mind for the scene he had just witnessed. His head was swimming he bent over and put his hands on his knees he tried to focus on his breathing. Abruptly, his mouth opened, and the entirety of his lunch flew out and landed on the floor before him. He heaved again, and again until there was nothing left to sick up. He wiped his mouth on the sleeve of his jacket and took a ragged breath.

Carl had never seen anything so sickening and disturbing in his entire life.

Avoiding the window on the door with his eyes, he made his way back to the entryway and sat down at the empty desk. He wasn't about to go into that room, not without talking to someone at headquarters. From what he could see, this was not a job that could be handled by one person.

He sighed and picked up the telephone receiver, time to get the big guns down here with the rest of the team. He would be out of his mind to deal with this situation alone.

∞

The air ducts were a maze of confusion, but somehow Brice felt he was making progress in his search. He had been searching all this time for Ariana, he knew, in his heart she was alive. Brice stopped to have a look at his knees. They were bleeding from crawling. He ripped strips of clothing in an attempt to wrap around his knees to use as padding.

Ariana jumped from a fitful sleep as she was startled, she heard a noise, and it sounded like something ripping. There it was again, terrified and determined she made her way towards the noise. Carefully Ariana peeked around the corner to see a figure in the duct. It seemed to be human. She thought as she let out a sigh of relief. She sat there watching. She had to make sure.

Trying to fight off a monster in the duct while unarmed would be a losing battle altogether. "Brice, is that you?" Ari asked with a hopeful tone.

"Ari, I found you." Brice turned in her direction, crawling at full speed. "I was so scared I would never see you again."

"You found me! You just wanted me to protect you!" Ariana said jokingly. Brice loved that fiery sarcasm. Admittedly he knew he was hooked. Ariana looked at Brice, thinking to herself. He cares about me, does he love me? I'm a strong independent career-driven woman. I don't have time for a boyfriend. What have I done? I made this man fall in love with me? Am I ready for love? It was then Ariana knew she was playing with fire, and she loved it. The two held each other tight, Ari began to cry, she was trembling, all these emotions coming over her at once. Brice had one hand on her back and the other on the back of her head, securing her tight to his chest. "It's going to be alright, we're together now," he said passionately.

Ari listened to his heartbeat, her breathing ragged, for the first time on the ship, she truly felt safe.

Brice put his hand under her chin, slowly lifting her face from his chest. When their eyes met, he wiped an escaping tear from her cheek with his thumb. His hand followed the contour of her chin to the back of her head. He slowly pulled her close, and their lips met, the passion overwhelming them both.

∞

George Meade sat in the bridge in the captain's chair

while those around him paced or cried. The noises outside the door had grown increasingly louder over the last couple of hours, and it was beginning to put his nerves on edge. It sounded like they were clawing their way through the door.

Here, he was surrounded by Rick Harris, Kevin Hines, and the hysterical stewardess Katy Richards. Still, he felt like he was the only one trying to do any real thinking. The others offered up nothing when he asked; all they gave him were bewildered looks.

"Okay, we know that their bodies are hard to kill," he started. "It seems to me that the answer is in that fact."

"What do you mean?" asked Kevin, giving the Captain's right-hand man his full attention.

George stood up. "Well, in case none of you have noticed these things are already dead. They are rotting and stinky, but they continue to be animated and reanimated. As long as they have a shell to walk around in, they survive and thrive."

"So?" Kevin said as he shrugged his shoulders.

George flashed him a look. "So that would tell me that the only way to defeat them is to completely destroy the body altogether."

"How the heck are we supposed to do that?" asked Katy. "Run them through a meat grinder? I'll bet they will all line up for that."

George smiled. "Fire."

Now he had everyone's attention. "We use fire to ward them off. We steer them into a common area and set them aflame."

"Thinking we could lure them anywhere is insane," replied Kevin. "They want to eat us. I've been doing the math, and I would say more than half of the passengers have turned into these things. How do you expect the four of us to be able to control this chaos long enough to save our own lives?"

Rick spoke up. "We would have to be sure we wouldn't burn up in the fire as well. We would have to have a safety zone determined, or we will end up jumping in the ocean and dying out there instead. You're not making sense, George."

Now George was getting frustrated. "I really don't see that we have a choice! The larger their numbers, the stronger they become. What do you want to do? Sit in here until they inevitably break through?"

No one answered him. "Fine," he continued. "I am going to figure out a solid plan. We have flares to light a fire. All we need now is teamwork and a good strategy."

Right then, there was a loud 'crack!' George knew right away that the sound was the door. It had likely weakened and cracked. "Listen, we can't be wasting any time. Let's put our heads together before it is too late!"

They huddled together and discussed the situation, as the pounding and tearing on the other side of the door continued.

∞

Brice was checking Ariana for wounds. "Let me have a look at that cut. It looks like it's going to need stitches, we need to get to my office. Can you crawl?"

"Yes, I can," Ari said with blushing cheeks.

The two made their way to the medical center, where Brice proceeded to tend to her wound. Ari watched as he worked on her injury. He touched her with such gentleness that it sent butterfly's fluttering through her stomach.

"I was climbing into the air duck when I caught my leg on a screw and ripped it open," Ari told Brice.

"I think we will be safe here for the night," Brice exclaimed.

"Look Brice, I know these ships have an armory. I need access." Together they worked a plan to get to the armory at daybreak.

The infirmary was quiet; the two were secure behind a locked door and bedding down for the night. Ariana was caressing her bandage, thinking to herself when she broke the silence. "I had to kill my mom," Ariana said bluntly. Brice sat up and watched as tears welled up in her eyes. All he could do was hold her and listen to the pain as it flowed from her voice.

The trauma of seeing your loved ones transformed into a vicious animal is undoubtedly a horrific moment. Brice was at a loss for words. What could he say, what could he do to lessen the pain. The truth was there was no way to unlive the moment she had. The terror will haunt her for the rest of her life. There was no choice; she had to face the facts. It seemed impossible to Brice that anyone could endure such pain without being plagued with nightmares for years to come.

"Ari," Brice said, as he held her tight. "The creature

you killed was no longer your mother. It was her body with bits and pieces of her memories." He paused as Ariana listened for him to continue. "It was using those memories to lure you in, to succumb to it. That's how it knew your name. Trust me. You did the right thing. I believe that's how McElroy can still pilot a vessel. There is just enough left in his decaying mind to recall such tasks, allowing them to hunt and feed. You will always have the good memories of your mother to hold on to. Don't let the recent event poison them."

The two were quiet for a moment digesting the words Brice said. "Look," he said, turning her to face him. "If I turn, don't listen to me, don't trust me. You have to stop me. Let me rest in peace; give me mercy." Brice said in a stoic tone. Then continued, "remember me the way I am right now."

∞

The Harrington boys, for the first time in any of their lives, were functioning as a team.

Sure, they were eating other humans and causing mass destruction, but they had never cooperated so fully with each other before. Jason, in his sick state of mind, found it wholly satisfying. Finally, his son obeyed him. Okay, granted, they all had to die and become zombies to get to this point, but he was pleased nonetheless.

Together they trolled the corridors of the ship, searching and smelling for fresh meat. They could smell it all around them, but tracking it down was a different story. The victims they were pursuing were creative when it came to dodging them and hiding. The fact was infuriating.

They continued on their venture, stopping only to have a fresh bite from a new victim whenever they found one. It was vital that they pressed on. After all, Captain McElroy promised that when they got to land, there would be more than enough fresh meat for everyone, and so, with that promise before them, Jason Harrington and his son hunted on.

Captain McElroy had left the destruction of the bridge door to the others. He wanted to check on the progress being made. He lurched around the ship and took stock. It appeared that they were experiencing success in wiping out the living. He couldn't see one living human in sight.

He began to shout, "We are coming! Hide if you like; there is no escape!"

After making his rounds, he returned to the bridge. He needed to be there when they finally broke through. That was the only way to guarantee that they would all make it to land. There was going to be plenty of fresh food once they docked.

When he reached the bridge, he fought his way through the others that were pounding at the door. He yelled, "George, I know you are there!"

The chief officer grimaced with fear. "What do I say?" he whispered.

"Answer him," Rick replied. "There is no reason to make him any angrier than he already is."

George stood and yelled at the door. "Yes sir, I am in here."

The captain laughed loudly and began to pound on the door again. "Never fear!" he yelled. "You will join us soon enough."

That's just what we're afraid of, Kevin thought to himself.

∞

Carl had gotten a hold of Clarissa and let her know that the Belize case was somewhat of an emergency. At first, his supervisor seemed skeptical, but when he told her the reality of what he had seen, the woman told him to hang tight. She wanted him to secure the building and wait for David Umbridge.

Carl was relieved they were sending in a seasoned expert; he was excited to work side by side with Umbridge. He put his gear back in the trunk of the rental car and shut it with a slam. He then took note of the alley once again. It wouldn't hurt to check things out right now before the team came. He wanted to see what kind of waste this place was producing, and he wanted to know if they had been taking the proper precautions in disposing of it.

He pulled a pair of rubber gloves out of his hip pocket and put them on as he walked down the alley. It was a dead-end with a brick wall closing it off. Up against the wall were two large dumpsters, and trash was all around them.

Carl noticed there was a back door to the lab. He trotted up three steps and tried the knob: locked. He resumed his mission and made his way to the dumpsters.

The first dumpster held nothing but typical garbage: food wrappers, disposable coffee cups, loads of used paper towels, and the like. As Carl was getting ready to shut the lid, he heard a weak squeaking sound coming from the other dumpster.

Carl stopped abruptly and listened hard. Yes, something was definitely in that dumpster. He cautiously walked over to it, and that was when he saw the dog.

The stray was mangled. It had to have been run over or beaten with something. It was covered in blood, and its legs were bent in unnatural positions. Tufts of fur were on the ground around it, and the bald patches in its skin looked as if they were rotting.

The critter opened one eye and whimpered at Carl.

"What the heck is going on here?" he asked himself in a low voice. Avoiding the rotting creature, Carl slowly began to lift the lid to the dumpster. Whatever was inside was becoming agitated. The sounds were growing increasingly louder. He took a small penlight from his pocket and carefully lifted the lid to see inside.

He was met with a scream that only a sick animal could produce. Inside the dumpster were countless rats, or at least, that's what he thought they were. Some were feasting on another pest in a corner while the others scurried around in confusion.

Carl dropped the lid. This was bad; this was really bad. If these things have been out here, there was an excellent chance that someone or something had become infected. He looked down at the mutt and shook his head.

The team needed to get here and fast.

He got in touch with local authorities. Within minutes, Belize police were pulling up; a man in uniform got out of the vehicle and approached him. When he reached him, he said with a thick accent.

"You are with American disease control?"

"Yes, we need to quarantine this building nobody in nobody out. Keep all citizens cleared from the streets and the area within the tape. I am going to pick up my associates, and we will be back in the morning." Carl had put caution tape across the mouth of the alley. It was bright red, and in black letters, it said 'Hazardous Waste: Do Not Enter.' He strung the tape across more than ten times.

∞

Tom and Red had just gone to the back of the fitness center and checked on the women and children. All had been fine, so he secured the door to the office area they were in and told the women to pile as much stuff against the door as possible. He let them know that Ron had left, and with any luck, they would be able to get safely out of here soon.

The two men went back out to the main area, where Jay was curled up in a corner with his hands over his ears sobbing. Tom shook his head in disgust. Jay was a blubbering grown man.

A loud crash came from the door, and the equipment they had used to barricade themselves, appeared to be moving slightly. The dead walkers moved there focus from the glass wall to the door. Tom stared at the entrance; there was a large crack running down the middle. It was compromised.

"C'mon!" He turned to the other two. "We don't have much longer to wait. They are going to get in." He paused and looked around. "Guys, help me put some more of this equipment against the door. It's all we can do."

Red got right to it, but Jay continued to cry and sob, his hands over his ears. Tom looked at Red, who shrugged in response. Best to do what they could, even if this crybaby was worthless.

They went about the task of reinforcing the entrance as best they could, but Tom knew it was just a matter of time. At least they could stall them this way. He glanced at his watch. Ron had been gone forty-five minutes. If he weren't back soon, Tom would make the decision to get everybody up into the air ducts and hope for the best.

It was the only option they had.

CHAPTER 16

David Umbridge was packing his bags on the bed, as his wife of 11 years walked in. "It's 8 pm and raining outside, where are you going?" She said with a puzzled look on her face.

"I have to fly to Belize for an investigation." He retorted as he zipped the inside pocket closed.

"An investigation?" She questioned emotionally fed up. "We haven't finished talking about us. Look, I probably won't be here when you get back, I can't do this any longer."

He glanced up from packing his bags. "It's my job, and you know this." He stated in a pleading voice as he closed the lid to his suitcase. "I've worked for the CDC, 19 years, and you ask me this every time. I'm trying to retire, and I have no choice, I have to go." And with that, he walked out the door.

David Umbridge, Keith Mitchell, and Kim Johnson sat in their seats on the jet, soaring over the rest of the planet. They were on a red-eye flight to Belize to join Carl Morgan. From the sounds of it, they were going to be in the middle of a big, confusing mess.

"Morgan says things are dying and coming back to

life," Umbridge was relaying. "I guess the issue is a result of some studies being done by some crazy doctor. At least, that's what Clarissa believed, just not in so many words. Morgan also said that he thinks we may be in trouble; he's never seen anything like the situation in Belize."

Kim spoke up. "So how do we handle a situation like this?" She was brand new to the CDC, and still wet behind the ears. "I mean, have you ever been in a similar situation? How can we go blindly into something we know nothing about?"

"Well," David replied, making sure both of the newbies were paying attention, "we will have to eradicate the vermin in question. We will be treating them much like we would treat smallpox or TB, only on a different level since they are 'living' creatures."

Keith said, "I would think it would be foolish for us to think we are going to wipe out the issue in one fell swoop. Let's be real here: we have no idea if this is contained in one building or if it has 'leaked out' or something. Dang, we don't know anything. Kim's right."

"I would tend to agree with you, but we have to try to get the job done with the tools we have been given." David leaned his head against the back of his seat and looked out the window at the night sky.

David had dealt with everything under the sun. He had dealt with the Ebola scare and the flesh-eating virus on more than one occasion. But in all his years with the CDC, he had never even heard of something like this.

Animal corpses coming back to life, eating and murdering each other, and then coming back to life again. It sounded like the very things nightmares were made of. It couldn't be real. There had to be some kind of mistake.

He looked over at his two associates. Both had their heads back, and their eyes closed. They were fresh-faced rookies; it made him smile as he recalled his humble beginnings. He just felt sorry for them that they were cutting their teeth on such an insane investigation as this.

Finally, he closed his own eyes and started to doze off. Better rest up now, he might not get another chance for a while.

∞

Ron Rogers sat on his rear end in the air duct. He felt completely powerless. Every grate he looked through showed him nothing but these dead cannibals. He had yet to see one living soul safe and sound. The zombies were making rapid progress indeed.

The problem he now faced was that he was utterly lost. Ron had tried to return to the fitness center and thought he knew the way. However, all he had been doing for the last half-hour was struggling to find his way back. He was scared stiff and had no idea what to do.

Panic was starting to rise inside of him. He was sitting across from a grate that led to a sauna room. He sat, staring out at a half-alive who was making a full meal of a naked man. The man seemed dead, and Ron was having a hard time dealing with the wet noises coming from the situation.

Right then, the naked man's leg jerked violently. He wasn't dead after all! Ron scooted closer to the vent just as the man grabbed the flesh-eating corpse and bit into its arm in return. Ron held his breath to keep from crying out. He wasn't dead, he was undead, and it had happened in a matter of minutes.

They were all in trouble. Ron was beginning to expect that they would never make it off the ship alive, but he knew they had to die trying. He backed away from the opening and began to get back into a crawling position. He had to find his way back to the fitness center.

As he positioned himself, he attempted to adjust quietly. Using his foot against the metal duct for footing, he sat up a bit to take off his overshirt. Right then, the rubber sole of his sneaker lost traction, and the rubber squealed against the metal with a loud 'screech!'

Ron froze and held his breath. He looked out the grate to see that both monsters were looking up at the vent, almost directly at him. Ron didn't move a muscle; he was petrified with fear.

The first zombie struggled to his feet. He didn't take his eyes off the grate, and he appeared to be smelling the air. He drew near to the vent along with the naked man, and both of them stopped right under the opening, their heads cocked back.

Unexpectedly the naked man, who was quite large and muscular, swung his fist at the duct and punched it with a bang. A significant dent formed just beneath Ron. He began to shake violently.

Now both of the wandering souls were punching. Large dents were appearing everywhere. He tried to crawl, but in his panic, he slid and hit his face hard on the duct. Blood spurted from his nose.

Another punch came, then another, and with that, a fist broke entirely through the metal. Ron curled up in a ball and tried to keep away from the fist. The supernatural grabbed the metal then and began to rip at it quickly, as though it were made of paper. The rotter tore it completely away, and Ron fell through onto the floor.

He didn't even have time to react. In seconds the half-deads were on him, tearing at his ligaments with their teeth. The last thought that went through his mind was, 'If you can't beat 'em, join 'em.'

∞

Another day had come and gone, and George was nearing the end of his rope.

While the other three with him at the bridge had all fallen asleep, he fought to stay awake. The zombies outside the locked and barricaded door had not let up, but they hadn't made further progress either. As for his plan, well, all he had accomplished for sure was the fact that they had flares. No one, including him, could figure out how to get out of the bridge and past the monsters. Surely, at least, one of them would die trying, if not all of them. George was familiar with every aspect of the ship, and he believed that without a map of the air ducts, one would certainly get lost. He said they would only succeed in dying of starvation in the vent instead of at the hands of the flesh-eaters. Since Brice hadn't returned, he was confident he met his demise.

George looked at his wristwatch: it was two-thirty in the morning. He stood and stretched and began to pace around the sleeping bodies of the others. He thought about Captain McElroy. The captain seemed all too patient with their defiance, and George had a feeling that this was a terrible sign.

The more he thought about it, the more he was convinced that they were not going to make it out of this alive. At the rate these things had taken over the ship, he assumed there was not a normal human passenger left, and if there was, they were going through exactly what George and his co-workers were going through on the bridge.

There has to be a solution. George thought to himself as he looked around. He thought long and hard about the air ducts. Brice thought it was a much more preferable way to go.

"We're not going to make it, are we George?" It was Katy. She was sitting up now, and she looked calmer than he had seen her since this all started.

He gave her a weak smile and said, "I don't know, Katy. I just don't know."

"I have to use the bathroom," she said.

George gave a slight chuckle. "Well, I'll turn around while you use the metal pail." They had all been using it, and the stench on the bridge was terribly foul, but what choice did any of them have?

He spun around in the chair and faced the wall. He heard Katy stream of urine start, and it seemed to go on forever. The girl must've been holding it for quite some time.

When she was finished, she said, "You can turn around now. Thank you."

He spun back around to see she returned to her spot on the floor. She was looking at him through the dimmed lights, and she said, "I'm starting to think that holing up in here is a futile means of saving ourselves. I've been thinking about jumping into the ocean and letting the chips fall where they may."

George raised his eyebrows. It almost seemed like a logical plan, but the fact was that they would die trying if they went that route. "It's no good, Katy," he said. "If the zombies don't get us, the sharks would."

"What about the idea with the flares," she continued. "Isn't there something we could do with the flares?"

Kevin gave a long, drawn-out sigh and shook his head. "I've been paying attention to the vent, but George says it's pointless. He's probably right when it comes down to it; he knows the ship far better than I do. It's just the only solution I can come up with, and it isn't a solution at all. It's a stall tactic."

Kevin wheeled one of the chairs over to the grate and stood on it. He could feel a slight breeze against his face, and he closed his eyes, letting himself enjoy the sensation for a minute. He hoped they made it through this alive.

The sounds from the other side of the door had grown louder now, which meant that Captain McElroy had returned to help the others break through the barricade. He listened with his eyes closed for the captain's maniacal laugh. Yep, there it is, he thought.

Maybe the best thing they could do was give up. It wasn't what Kevin wanted to do, but it was the only thing that made sense. Had this situation occurred on land, they would have had a chance. There were endless places to hide and even more means of escape. But it didn't happen on land. It was happening in the middle of the Ocean.

Kevin plopped down into the chair he had been standing on and put his head in his hands.

"Death doesn't like to be stalled," Katy said quietly. With that, she lay back down on the floor with her back to Kevin, and in the dim light, he could see her shoulders heaving; she was quietly crying.

George glanced at Kevin with a futile look, then leaned back in the chair and closed his eyes once again as he listened to the zombies on the other side. No new ideas would come. The only way out seemed to be to give in. Katy was more right than she knew: death did not like to be stalled.

∞

Carl Morgan sat in his hotel room in the dark. He couldn't pry his mind away from what he had seen in the alley. Never had he encountered such freaks of nature as those that were scurrying in the dumpster.

Carl looked at the alarm clock near the bed: four-thirty in the morning. The team would be arriving in Belize at six, and he was to be there to greet them. They would all go directly to the site and decide how it should be dealt with.

Carl rose and went into the bathroom for a shower. He took his time in the steaming water, and it helped to clear his head a bit. Now all he needed was an insanely strong cup of coffee. Carl hadn't slept well last night. Every time he closed his eyes, he dreamed of deformed rats and dead bodies that moved on their own.

He got out of the shower and dried off and dressed. Once he was all put together, he left the room, and then he bought a stiff cup of java to take with him to the airport. He was so relieved that the team would finally be here. The situation waiting for them was going to blow their minds.

At the airport, he parked the rental and then went in to meet the team. He stood, coffee in hand, watching each and everyone as they got off the plane. Eventually, a trio consisting of two men and one woman approached him.

"Carl Morgan?" the taller man asked.

"Yes," he nodded and held out his hand to shake. "I'm Carl Morgan."

The man took his hand and nodded. "I'm David Umbridge," he said, then he gestured to the other two with a nod of his head. "These are my teammates: Kim Johnson and Keith Mitchell."

"David, your reputation precedes you," Carl said as

he shook David's hand. "It is a pleasure to work with you finally. My rental car is parked outside, but I think we should trade it in for a van. You have all of your equipment, I presume?"

Keith answered, "Yes. We need to get it from the carousel."

"Fine," Carl replied. "If you want to go do that, I'll go trade in the car. Meet me at the rental place when you are done? Then I can brief you on the situation during the drive."

They separated, and Carl headed to the Car Rental outfit. He had a large van secured under the CDC in no time, and soon all four of them were driving to the lab site.

"Well," Carl began, "I guess I'll start from the beginning. I'm sure you have been given reports regarding the initial call we received. Bruce West was the lab assistant to one Dr. Jonathan Anson. The two of them are American."

Kim spoke for the first time. "So, what were they doing down here?"

"According to the report Bruce West gave HQ, he and Dr. Anson had gotten into some sticky trouble in the states. They were working on a serum to prolong life, or eradicate death, whatever you prefer," he paused and cleared his throat. "They were illegally testing on animals, so they came here to continue their work without stirring up problems for themselves."

"So, what happened?" asked Keith. "Poison gasses?"

Carl kept his eyes on the road and shook his head. "From the looks of it, their studies were successful. They did indeed learn how to prolong life, or so it appears. The issue lies in what else they succeeded in doing."

He went quiet as his mind turned to the bodies on the floor, struggling to rise and live again. "They created monsters," he stated simply.

"Monsters?" David asked. "What the heck are you talking about?"

He glanced at the man out of the corner of his eye and offered him a weak smile. "They have injected rats with a serum that enabled them to come back to life after they die. The problem is they are violent and hungry. They eat each other, and even then, the victim returns to life."

"My," Kim whispered under her breath.

Carl looked at her in the rearview mirror. "As you will soon see."

David Umbridge had been with the Centers for Disease Control for nineteen years, and with each passing year, he found himself more and more excited about his retirement. It had been a good stretch, but the more sickness he saw, the more he began to hate his job. Now here he was, trolling down the streets of Belize in a rental car, heading to the lab of some mad scientist who had taken his hopes and dreams a little bit too far.

They arrived at the brick building within a half-hour. All of them got their equipment from the van and headed toward the building. Carl waved to the officer signifying his return. When they reached the door, Carl turned to them. "Wait," he said. "I changed my mind. I think I should show you the dumpster first."

The group went down the front steps, gear in hand, and walked over to the mouth of the alley. Carl took a knife from his pocket and cut through the strands of red tape, then gestured with his head for them to follow him.

"I initially went down here, because it was obvious that one of the dumpsters went to this building," Carl said. "I was curious as to what they were disposing of, as well as how they were disposing of it."

As they neared the dumpster, Kim stopped suddenly. "Do you hear a squeaking noise?"

Her two associates listened carefully, and then Carl spoke up. "You all should. That's what I want to show you."

He stopped in front of the dumpster and pointed to the mangled dog first. "I don't know how he is alive, but he doesn't seem able to die. He's a mess."

They stared at the horrible site for only a moment before Keith said, "I need to get some samples."

"Hold on," Carl replied. "I want to show you this first. Then you can take all the samples you like."

With that, he turned on his penlight and opened the lid. He aimed the light down into the container to show the others what was inside. All of them stopped breathing.

"What the heck?" David's voice sounded both

confused and sick.

"Are they sick? What are they?" asked Kim.

Carl let the lid down. "They are rats that have died and reanimated over and over again."

"How do you know this?" asked David.

Carl laughed and shook his head. He felt like he was going crazy. "When you see what is inside, you'll know how I came to that conclusion."

David looked around, thinking there was no way to know if anyone in Belize had encountered one of these animals. That's when he noticed the cameras. He knew that this situation had the potential to be quite destructive. These crazy people had not practiced any type of containment policy. They had simply thrown these rats in the trash and hoped for the best.

David took the lead and instructed his team, "Grab your collection samples, and let's make it a point to back up the mainframe and surveillance footage when we get inside." Pointing to the surveillance cameras on the side of the building as he spoke.

After about 20 minutes, the four of them made their way back to the front door. All of them were sick with disgust. From the looks of it, they had a serious dilemma on their hands.

∞

By the time the two zombies in the sauna ate their fill of Ron Rogers, he had started coming back around. They had managed to rid him of most of the blood in his body, along with his left forearm and right kidney, but what the heck, he didn't need it anymore.

Now Ron was struggling to stand, and the naked man helped him to his feet. He pointed to the air duct, and in a thick slow voice, asked, "Where does this lead?"

Ron looked up at the gaping hole and smiled. "Anywhere we want," he replied.

The clumsy beasts fought their bodies to do what they wanted them to do. The one who had made a meal of Naked Sauna Man said, "I want to get up there."

The other two assisted the first one, and then the muscular sauna guy helped by boosting Ron up. Finally, the other two reached down and pulled him up along with them.

"We can get anywhere in the ship through here," Ron told them. "I know where there is enough fresh meat to last a long, long time."

With that, he began to lead, and suddenly it seemed he knew his way through the ducts as if he had been born there. He knew he had gotten lost before, but his dead mind did not understand how. The reality was he was going by smell, and he could smell better than ever. He smelled people. Grown-ups and children alike.

They trudged along, one after the other, and they paid no mind to the amount of noise they made. There was no place for the people to hide even if they did hear them coming.

Tom stood under the grate and listened carefully. He thought he could hear Ron up there, but he couldn't be sure. Tom had attached and secured the vent after an hour, just as Ron had told him to. Now he was waiting to see if the man was going to return at all.

He had checked on the women and children an hour ago and let them use the restroom in small groups. Now they were all asleep, as were Red and the guy who cried all the time. He was the only creature stirring inside the fitness center.

He and Red had piled everything possible in front of the cracked door. He could still hear the monsters clawing and pounding and screaming their guttural sounds, but the door had not given any more. He even thought that the sound of them had lessened. Maybe they were finally going away.

Tom slid down the wall and bent his knees, so he had a place to rest his arms and head. He was so tired he couldn't think straight, but someone had to be responsible. He knew neither Red nor Crybaby was capable.

He had just begun to doze off when he heard an echo coming from the vent. It sounded like someone was crawling towards it. It had to be Ron!

Tom stood up and pressed his ear against the wall to hear the sounds more clearly. Sure enough, someone was coming toward them in the air shaft! He grabbed the trash can they had been standing on and put it under the opening. Then he stood on it on his tip-toes and peered through the very bottom, and he could only do that just barely.

He was squinting, struggling to see anything he could through the darkness. The sound of Ron didn't sound like before. There was much more of an echo, almost like there was someone with him.

Tom's heart stopped as the truth became clear. They had gotten to Ron, and he was bringing others back to get at all of them. He stepped down from the pail and looked around the room for something, anything, that would act as some kind of weapon.

All of the equipment was state-of-the-art. Not even a weight on a rope existed in here. There were exercise balls that would be useless. There were some jump ropes. Other than that, Tom was empty-handed.

He looked back up at the grille, his eyes wide. They were getting closer. All he could think of to do was shut the door in there and then pile stuff up on the outside, just as they had done with the main entrance. He locked the door and shut it tight, then went out into the main fitness area.

"Hey! Red, I need you to wake up! I need your help," He was shaking Red hard, and in less than a minute, the man opened his eyes and looked at Tom with confusion.

"Wha-what?"

"I think they got Ron. They are coming this direction through the grates. I need you to help me barricade the storage door," He stood up and tapped his foot restlessly as Red struggled to clear his head. "Now! They are almost here! I could hear them!"

The two men set about piling what they could in front of the door, even moving a large desk from one of the offices. Soon the door could not be seen, but they were completely out of materials with which to barricade another door if they needed to.

They stood there quietly, both men wide awake, watching the door, and listening. In only a couple of minutes, they heard the pounding begin on the weak metal grille. They looked at each other with dismay.

"Tommy, Tommy!" It was Ron's voice, only it was thick and garbled, as though he was trying to speak around a mouthful of food. "Help a brother out, Tommy!"

The banging became more insistent, and after less than five minutes, they heard it break away altogether. "We're coming to get you, Tommy!"

Something inside of Tom snapped right then. He began to laugh hysterically, and he sat down hard right in the middle of the hallway where they stood.

"Tom," Red said. "You have to pull yourself together!"

Tom stopped laughing just long enough to respond. "Yes! We will pull ourselves together, so we are fit to be torn apart."

That was when the last of his sanity left him for good.

R.W.K. Clark

CHAPTER 17

The Fantasy Lines cruise ship was cutting through the ocean water like a hot knife in butter. It was dark out, with only the light of the moon coming from the sky. The ship was lit up, and if someone were watching the goings-on, they would have gone into cardiac arrest.

On every level, there was violence and murder taking place. People ate their mothers and fathers; others ate their children. The language being spoken was nothing more than grunts or groans between the monsters, but they were capable of speaking to the living in English, and that they did.

The zombies wanted to take over the entire ship, and they intended to dock it and do the same when they got to land. It was chaos in the meantime, with nothing more than blood and violence going on.

Those in hiding knew that there was no escape. They knew that they would die trying. There was nothing else they could do unless they wanted to become someone's next meal.

Several passengers had jumped off the ship into the ocean in an effort to save their own lives. Not one survived, that took this route. They all ended up drowning, and that served to piss off Captain McElroy to no end. What a waste of perfectly good food.

∞

It was early in the morning, Ariana and Brice were crawling through the ventilation shaft, making their way to the armory. Brice's mind turned to the scientific aspects of the mess they were in. How had this happened? What had caused the terrible transformations? The doctor in him was on the verge of insanity, trying to figure it out. He shook his head and groaned with frustration.

"We're here, I'm over the security office, and I hope the keys are in here, somewhere," Brice whispered as he looked at Ari. "The armory is that door there behind the desk." He said, pointing through the vent. Quietly he opened the grille and lowered himself onto the desk. Within moments Ari was next to him. They proceeded to search the office for a spare key.

∞

Captain James McElroy had taken a break from beating on the entry to the bridge. That cat and mouse game was getting old. The only reason he wanted in so badly, had nothing to do with his need for food. He simply wanted to make sure they docked. There would be plenty of food to spare if they did.

The captain was sitting in his chair in the cabin he had once shared with his wife, and he was eating the flesh off some guy's calf as though it were a chicken leg. The man had turned shortly after McElroy killed him, and now he was somewhere on board crawling around on his hands and knee. It entertained him to think that this little 'family' was growing at such a wonderful pace.

Satisfied, he tossed the calf into a corner of his cabin. Now his mind went back to the bridge. Damn George Meade! He should have been the first one to be taken care of. He had the knowledge and experience needed to take them to safety. But McElroy didn't care; as long as they docked, everything would be just fine.

He struggled with his mind as he tried to deduce who all was on the bridge. He was pretty sure Dr. Brice Cummings was because he hadn't seen him since this started. Whoever else was in there were individuals he had taken no real notice of on the ship, to begin with, so he wasn't worried about them. McElroy was, however, worried about Meade and Cummings. He had to get in the bridge!

He stood from his place, stumbling as he tried to get his footing. His left leg didn't seem to be working all that well. Rigor mortis had actually set in, and he found the burden of it put a wrench in his spokes. He reached up to straighten his captain's hat, and as he did, his hand brushed against his forehead. A layer of skin sloughed off of him and fell to the floor. He paid it no mind.

He was ready to take the upper hand. He knew they were down to the brass tacks when it came to passengers. The only humans left on board were a large group in the fitness area, and the staff holed up on the bridge. Yes, they were certainly getting down to it. They would have to save some of the humans and make them last until they docked if they wanted to squash their incessant hunger.

He decided he would address those who were trying to get inside the fitness center. He would give them specific directives only to bite and infect the others, not to indulge too much. He didn't know if it would work, considering that the hunger seemed to take over their entire beings, but they had to be told. Then he would do the same with those outside the bridge.

He loped up the corridor to the elevator, dragging his right leg behind him. He stepped inside and pushed the button, and then he rested his weight against the wall. His stomach growled obnoxiously.

Oh, he could hardly wait to dock. It would be like a buffet. He smiled a rotten smile.

The world and everything in it would be theirs.

The only problem he could foresee, and that not clearly due to his state, was the lack of fresh flesh on the ship. The captain knew they were all starting to dine on each other, and the result was less than desirable. They needed meat, and they needed it soon. They were going to have to get to those in hiding, and they needed to do it fast.

∞

George and Kevin were trying to come up with a solution, any solution, to the predicament they were in.

"I don't understand, George," Kevin said. "We are in the very area that controls the ship. Why don't we just skip docking the boat?"

George shook his head vigorously. "For one thing,

we will be out in the middle of the ocean, with no help and no way to get any. Right now, we have half a chance to get to land and escape their clutches. We may be able to ward them off, or we can hope, at least."

"But if we skip docking, we can be sure that these monsters won't be able to hurt anyone else," Kevin continued.

"Look," George replied with a firm, steady voice. "I want to survive, and you want to survive. If we skip docking, there is no chance of survival whatsoever. Sure, the boat will be in the middle of the ocean, but we don't know if these animals can even be killed, much less die because they are out of food." He shook his head again.

Staying barricaded on the bridge was not the solution either, and he knew it. It was only a matter of time before they got to them. One of them needed to buck up and attempt to get out and get a lifeboat to land. Someone had to do it.

George began to sort out a plan that would give them half a chance. He was sure he could think of something.

∞

The armory was not what Ariana expected. Mostly flairs and a few sidearms. Hardly any ammunition just spools of razor wire. "That's it?" Ariana questioned. "How are we going to fight off all the zombies with a fraction of the ammo we need?"

Brice was dumbfounded at the stockpile before him. He hoped for more, at least some assault weapons would have been nice.

Their plans to take over the ship quashed.

Ariana broke the silence, "Looks like we have six hundred rounds of 9mm, to kill off 3000 walking corpses." Ariana said as she looked up at Brice, holding some rounds in her hand. "We need another plan."

∞

Tom had begun laughing. At first, his laughter consisted of nothing more than a few giggles, and those only came when he made out Ron's voice on the other side of the door. They had gotten Ron, which meant they would get him, Red, and the others. The thought, for some reason, struck him as hilarious. The central fitness aria had been compromised, so Tom and Red locked themselves in a small office.

That was when his laughter took control, having fits of giggles. Red stared at him, mouth open.

"What are you doing, Tom?" he asked slowly.

Tom turned to him, his eyes wild. "If you can't beat 'em, join 'em."

Red stood up slowly, keeping a firm eye on Tom as he did. The dude had lost it, that much was obvious. Now it sounded like he wanted to let the walking flesh eaters in and have a potluck with them. There was no way he was going to let that happen; no way at all.

Red felt a tinge of panic; he had to stop him, but Tom was a lot tougher than he was. He looked around nervously, and that was when he saw a metal pole standing in the corner behind a couple of boxes.

He walked up to it and grabbed it; it had some

weight to it, even though it was hollow in the middle. It was obviously steel. Red knew it was part of a barbell set, and it would do the trick. He turned to Tom. "Tom, I'm gonna ask you to stop that dude, just sit there and be quiet," he said, trying to sound as authoritative as possible. Tom turned and looked at him, laughing.

Red had to do it. He built up his courage, at least as much as he could muster up, then he walked up to Tom, and without a second thought, Red swung the pole. It hit Tom in the head with a thick metallic sound, and Tom hit the floor. His hand went to the back of his head, and when he pulled it away, it was covered in blood.

"I told you to quit it," Red said. "I'll hit you again if I have to."

Tom lay on the floor with a dazed look on his face. Red stood over Tom, who had started laughing again.

"They're going to get us," Tom said.

Right then, a child started to cry loudly. It was obviously one of the children locked in the office with the women, across the hall from them. For a fraction of a second, the monsters stopped their pounding and listened.

A garbled voice yelled. "More meat! Down here!"

Their footsteps then began to shuffle toward the large office. They were going to the women and children! They would not be able to protect themselves; there was absolutely no way!

"Damnit, we have to stop them," Red said. "We can't let this happen."

Tom just lay on the floor, bleeding and laughing, he was worthless at this point. Red knew he couldn't just stay in here and listen to the monsters killing and eating the women and kids. He had to do something.

Heck with it, he thought, he couldn't live with himself if he survived and women and children died. No way.

He was going to go out there fighting.

∞

The father-son duo, was none the less, a tag team feeding frenzy of mass destruction. Jason thought about his little Sunshine. He was sure his beautiful Ariana was starving by now. Jason knew she wouldn't do the killing herself, so he was more than ready to provide fresh nourishment to his wonderful daughter. He would save a bite for Ari. He grunted to Adam as he popped an eyeball from the woman they were feasting on. Adam saw the eyeball in Jason's hand as he went to place it in his shirt pocket. "No, for Ariana," Jason said in an animalistic voice as he swatted Adam's hands away from the delightful snack. "We must find Ariana."

∞

The four CDC agents had suited up in protective gear and were now standing in the waiting area of the brick building. Carl Morgan was filling them in on what they would see when they went into the hallway to the lab. He didn't think all the briefings in the world would truly prepare them, but at least he could say he tried.

"When I first got here, I gave this area a look

around," he began. "No one was at the desk; the place appeared to be empty. But then I went through that door, and that was when I heard the noises."

Keith cleared his throat. His eyes looked nervous, and he appeared to be working hard at keeping it together. "So what the heck is back there? What did this Jonathan Anson do?"

"Well, as far as I can tell, he succeeded in defeating death, at least to a certain degree," Carl replied. "The test rats have obviously been doing the same thing as the vermin in the dumpster. They seem to have been eating each other and then resurrecting, over and over again."

Now Kim spoke up. "So, we are going to see a bunch of cannibalistic mice."

"Yes," Carl said. "But more than that, you are going to see Bruce West and some woman, I assume the secretary, being eaten, and they are, or were, in the middle of coming back too."

"Who knows what a re-animated human is capable of," said David. He took a deep breath. "Okay, let's do this thing."

With Carl in the lead, the four of them went through the entrance marked 'Restricted.' They skipped looking in the other doors and walked directly to the lab. Carl looked in first.

"I only see Bruce West," he said. "Where is that woman?"

He stepped back and let Keith look through the window. West was staggering, literally in circles, and he was all but covered in the chewing, gnawing lumps of skin and hair that had once been rats. Keith gagged and staggered back from the door, allowing Umbridge to step up.

"Unbelievable," David said. "It seems he is trying to make his way to the door, but he's not having much luck."

Something clanged behind them. It sounded like metal hitting the floor. All four of them turned around.

Behind them stood the woman. She was hardly recognizable as a human being. The four gawked at her in shock, mouths open and eyes wide. She opened her mouth and let out a nearly deafening screech. Then she lurched forward, arms twitching and flailing around.

David was the only agent that was armed, and that's because he was licensed to carry at all times. He was never without a gun, but the others had no desire, or need, for one. At least not until today. David realized that the weapon was nestled under the protective gear, and he had no idea how to get to it quickly.

As the dead woman lurched toward them, they were walking backward. They went only a few feet before they hit the back wall. There was no place for them to run to.

David reached up and unzipped the front of his gear, then reached inside and got the gun out of his holster. With his eyes frozen on the unknown woman, he let the safety off and aimed the gun right at her head. Before anyone could think, he pulled the trigger.

The bullet hit the woman's head dead center, leaving

a neat little hole in the front and splattering brains all over the wall behind her. She hit the floor like a bag of sand. They all continued to stare at her.

"You got her," Kim said. "She's not moving; do you think she's dead?"

"I don't know," David replied.

Keith crept forward until he was only a couple of feet from her rat chewed corpse, then he looked down at her face with its eyes wide open. "I think she may be dead."

Keith knelt to get a closer look. Suddenly it looked as if she jerked, and a rat flew out of her blouse and was on him just that fast. He had hit it swinging his arms in the air, as the vermin's teeth bit into his collar, ripping a piece from him.

David, Kim, and Carl sprang into action. They all grabbed hold of Keith, who was screaming as the little beast bit into his neck. They continued to pull on him even as blood shot from his wound like a geyser.

David thought he is already as good as dead.

The three of them combined were no match for the rat as it scurried around after everyone's feet. It had turned its full attention to Kim, who was screaming bloody murder as she backed into the corner. Instantly the pest ran up her leg and bit into her hand. David grabbed Carl by the shoulder and pulled him back out of the way to clear a line of sight to fire at the vermin. The rat blew apart in little pieces when the projectile hit.

Keith was unconscious, and Kim was holding her bleeding hand. David immediately grabbed the trauma kit from his hip to tend to Kim and directed Carl to check the data closet behind them. "Carl, grab what you can quickly!" he exclaimed. "We have to get out of here!"

Kim's head was swimming, and she felt like she was going to pass out. She was speaking, but the words didn't make sense to David. He watched as her eyes roll back. In seconds he had a blood collection tube in her vein and was collecting a sample. Carl startled him from behind, causing him to jerk the collection tube from her arm, his heart was pounding. "You scared the hell out of me," he said, looking up at Carl.

"Let's go I've got all the external drives including the surveillance." Carl stated, then quickly grabbed David by the shirt, pulling him backward. Just in time to save David from Kim's snapping teeth that came within inches of his face.

They went through the door that led to the entryway and slammed it shut behind them. Then they moved the massive oak desk in front of it, and leaned their backs against it and stopped to catch their breath. All they could hear from the other side of the door was Kim's screams and some distant wet noises.

There was a small square window in this door, just as in the others, but it was covered over with heavy brown construction paper. Carl got on the desk on his knees and began to claw at the tape that held the brown paper in place. Soon it was ripped away.

"They're eating each other," he said, his voice trembling.

David got on the desk. "What do you see? Move aside, Morgan."

Carl sat back on his rear, his eyes distant and confused. David looked through the window to see that Keith was already jerking around, while the unknown woman lay immobile on her back being eaten by Kim.

"Keith is trying to sit up," David said in a stunned voice. "He is trying to stand up, Carl!"

"He is reanimating," Carl said as he stared at nothing. "I tried to tell you; this is what happens."

David turned to him, his eyes wild. "Well, we have to figure it out, and now!" He looked back through the window just in time to see Kim flailing her arms. She was getting up. As for the unknown woman, she is not moving, perhaps a shot to the head is the only solution to kill these things.

"We have to burn this place to the ground," David said finally.

That got Carl's attention. Of course! If they burned them, there would be no bodies left to reanimate. He didn't know if it would work, but it sounded like the only thing that might.

"I'm going to call HQ and tell them what we've got," David continued, his face filled with fear. "If they want us to handle it any other way, I will likely not follow orders. I'm burning this place to the ground."

David got off the desk and unzipped his suit. He then stepped out of it and left it on the floor in a pile. He picked up the receiver to the phone that had been on the desk and dialed the CDC headquarters.

"Clarissa, it's David Umbridge," he said into the receiver. "I need to speak to Ray Ashton."

After a few moments of silence, he spoke again. "Ray? It's David Umbridge. I'm here in Belize, and we have a situation."

CHAPTER 18

Captain James McElroy stood at the furthest point out on the deck. From there, he was able to look up and get a good idea of what his walking dead horde was doing on each and every level. McElroy could see that they were busy, very busy indeed. While he was unable to see every shop or facility, he knew that each one was loaded with them, and they were doing an excellent job of feeding themselves and making more.

He was ravenous, and they had eaten nearly every fresh human on the ship. As he stood there, he caught a strong whiff of fresh blood. Where was that coming from? Were there still humans to be had?

He began his jerky walk in the direction of the scent. As he neared it, he realized all of the zombies were working their way in the same direction. Excluding the ones on the bridge. The humans he smelled were likely the last on the ship, and he wasn't about to share anything he got with the others.

He was heading up the main corridor that led to the fitness center. The smell was so intense that it was making his mouth pucker. In his decaying mind he had nearly forgotten about all the fresh human's, ripe for the pickings. The front of the fitness center was covered in immortals. The captain was forced to throw them, one at a time, away from the entrance. He got into the main area, and all the walkers were crowded around a door in the back.

That was where the meat was. McElroy could smell the aroma as if it was right in front of him.

He started up the short hall toward the office where the women and children were. Wandering corpses were banging at the door, and ripping and clawing at the walls, and they were doing damage. He could hear women screaming and children crying, and the sounds made him more eager to dine than ever.

He passed a door on his right, and that was when he heard talking. He turned to see an entry right next to him, and he reached out to the handle. It was locked. He pressed his ear to the door and listened.

"Tom, get up! The women and children are in trouble," a voice said. "You need to help me get this barricade down so we can help them."

"I'm not helping anybody," a voice replied. "I'm staying right here." The voice gave way to crazy laughter.

The captain could hear things being moved around in the room. "Suit yourself, you vile pain in the rear!"

That is when the captain realized that whoever was inside this room was taking down the barricade they had built!

He moved to the side of the door. He would stand there patiently. In a very short time, he would have something fresh to eat.

∞

Ariana was brainstorming ideas. "We can't let the ship dock. There must be a way to stop this thing? Perhaps there is a compromise. We could get close enough to drop anchor, at least then we would have a swimming chance." She continued, "We could have the ship quarantined a safe distance away, without risking the mainland, and countless lives."

Brice looked at Ariana as if a lightbulb went off. "That's a great idea. Who's to say these animals can't run a lifeboat, more or less swim?" Brice paused for a moment, then continued. "Well, their movement is slow, I think with their limited speed and motion they would be hard-pressed to keep afloat."

Ariana spoke up. "True, it would be easier for us to stop one dinghy at a time than the entire passenger load."

His head was slowly nodding in agreement, as he expressed. "Okay, let's program the autopilot to stop the ship one mile from the harbor. We could safely jump overboard and swim for land."

∞

David was wrapping up his phone call with Ray at the CDC headquarters. He related everything that he knew, in great detail, regarding the situation in Belize. It seemed pretty grim, and they could only hope that no one outside of the lab had been infected, but right now, there was no way of knowing. Ray made it perfectly clear the word zombie would not be used on a report.

He hung up the phone and looked at Carl. "We are to torch this place. All of it."

"With what?" Carl asked.

David turned his attention to the banging on the restricted door that had just begun. They were trying to get through. "Ray is letting the authorities know we need dynamite, and we need it now."

The two men went out of the main entry and put their backs against it. The last thing they needed was for these living corpses to get out of the restricted area, then they would be able to get to the street. David and Carl signaled to the officers for help; they all had to keep them inside until more help arrived.

After about ten minutes, they heard a loud 'crack' from inside. David opened the main entrance and looked inside. "The door... they are causing damage. We are not going to be able to keep them down much longer, Carl."

"I know," he replied. "But I think help has arrived."

David turned around to see two fire trucks and more Belize police pulling up. Two of the police cars were regular cars with lights on top, but the third was an unmarked unit. A man in a suit got out of the vehicle and approached them. When he reached the two, he said with a thick accent, "You two are with American disease control?"

"Yes," David said quickly, extending his hand to the man. "We have a bit of a problem here."

The three men talked briefly about the situation. The

policeman, whose name was Baros Abana, related to the men what Ray from the CDC had told him over the phone, and they confirmed all of it.

"You'll excuse me," Officer Abana said, "but I am having a hard time believing you. It all seems like a made-up tale."

David nodded. "I know, but it is real nonetheless."

From the inside, there was yelling and screaming that was completely unintelligible, and the door was cracking, getting weaker and weaker with every hit it took.

"As you can see, we have very little time," Carl said. "If they get out, we will never be able to get the situation under control."

Abana turned around and motioned for two of his men to join them. Both men carried large black canvas bags. "These men will handle the setup and detonation of explosives. We will get down to it now."

He then turned to his men. "Secure all six units to this building, and make sure you do it all around. We need to be certain the problem inside is eliminated."

The men nodded and left them to get things going. As they worked, Carl, David, and Abana talked about the issue, David explained his theory of stopping the animals with a headshot. About ten minutes in, the men heard a deafening crash from inside the building. Abana looked through the window, and his eyes grew wide. He looked panicked but soon pulled himself together. He ran for the men who were setting up the explosives and yelled something. Then he ran back to Carl and David, who were struggling to hold the door shut with their bodies.

"They will detonate in two minutes. We must keep the monsters inside until they give us the word." Abana leaned his own body against the door to help the others keep it shut, freeing David's hands enough to finish wrapping chain around the handles.

Less than two minutes later, the explosive experts came running. As they passed, one of them yelled at Abana. "Come on now!"

Abana yelled. "We must get across the street to safety!"

They bolted down the handful of steps and ran across the street where all the other officials were waiting. Citizens had been cleared from the streets, and the area was cordoned off with tape. There were sharpshooters posted all around the perimeter.

"Three, two, one!" The bomb specialist pushed down the plunger with force, and the dynamite blew.

∞

Drops of sweat trickled down Brice's temples and ran over his cheeks. He wiped at it with his forearm and continued moving. He and Ariana had been crawling through the air ducts for hours, and they had yet to find one single room that was not occupied by one or more zombies.

Brice wasn't sure of the route he should take; he was moving forward depending totally on his sense of direction. The only problem was that his sense of direction seemed to be a bit off. More than once, Brice thought he was where he needed to be, only to discover he was nowhere near the Bridge. It was more challenging to navigate the ducts than he could've imagined.

He came to an L-shaped corner with a grate. He stopped and looked out of it to see two of the monsters dining on shreds of flesh. At least that was what it looked like. It certainly didn't look human. He watched in horror as the thing they were eating began to struggle. Brice thought he would wretch then and there.

He tore his eyes away from the grisly scene and took off his button-down shirt. He folded it like an accordion length-wise and tied it around his head. That will help with the sweat, he thought, and I'll be much cooler in just a t-shirt. Ariana sat beside him, looking out at the living dead feasting below. "It's a child," she said in horror, as she put her hand to her mouth in disgust.

Brice was just getting ready to turn to the left when he heard the gurgling voice of a rabid evil spirit. "Blood."

Brice backed up a bit and looked out the grate again. One of them had its nose in the air. It was apparent, Brice thought as his heart skipped a beat. "They can smell us." He whispered to Ariana.

No one had taken notice of his scent as of yet, and he had given the situation little thought. But now the animated corpse who was smelling the air was standing, as was the other with it. The rotter's eyes were open, and it was still sniffing and walking in the direction of the air ducts.

Ariana didn't hesitate. She started to crawl, not making any noise. She could hear the zombies below Brice, and it was all she could do just to keep ahead of them.

Brice and Ariana took a right and picked up their pace a bit. Suddenly she stopped; she couldn't hear them anymore. They had lost them.

∞

"I'm not going with you," Tom was saying, over and over to Red. His voice was hysterical, and his eyes were wild.

Red was disgusted. "I don't care what you do." He bent down and picked up the metal rod he had hit Tom with.

"I'm going to go out swinging. If you are staying, barricade the door behind me." He paused, then said, "Wish me luck."

"Whatever," Tom replied, laughing. "You're an idiot."

Red looked away from him and positioned the pole on his shoulder. He took a deep breath and opened the door. Just as he said, when he stepped through the threshold, he started swinging the pole violently.

The zombies were all trying to claw their way into the office where the women and children were. Red could hear their screams and cries. He kept swinging as he took a right. Suddenly someone had hold of him; a tight grip indeed.

He dropped the pole, and it hit the floor. Red tried to see who had him in such a powerful bear hug, but he knew it didn't matter. Teeth came down on his shoulder just as the other immortals took notice of the fresh food that was so easily accessible behind them. They forgot about the women and children in the office, if only for a moment.

Then they were on him, biting and chewing, ripping him limb from limb.

R.W.K. Clark

CHAPTER 19

The explosion that occurred when they detonated the dynamite at the laboratory was intensely powerful. The streets and surrounding buildings shook with great severity. Even those who were standing in the safe range were shaken off their feet.

Dust flew, and flames shot around everywhere. Authorities and other onlookers were far enough away to spare their lives but close enough to get covered in the resulting debris. David, Carl, and Officer Abana scanned the site with their eyes before they even considered approaching. The single building that was next door to the location suffered extensive damage as well, but otherwise, the neighborhood remained intact.

"Abana, please radio your soldiers, make sure your snipers are ready. I believe a headshot is a sure way to stop a rotter from advancing. In addition, make sure your firefighters are ready with the flame throwers, for any other biological matter." David voiced with surety.

"Do you see anything?" Carl asked. The dust and debris had cleared reasonably well, though it did seem to take a lot of time. The three men and a group of ready firefighters were slowly approaching.

David grunted. "I don't see anything but a major mess."

They began to walk around the perimeter of the building. Bricks lay in heaps, and drywall was flaming. The men were all coughing from the pollution that had been released into the air.

"Wait," Officer Abana said anxiously. "In that place there." He pointed his finger toward the rear of where the building used to stand.

A massive section of smoldering drywall was moving up and down, as though an animal was trying to free itself.

"We need flames.!" Abana yelled. "Bring them in!"

A group of around eight firefighters marched in carrying what looked to be large guns. Each ran around the debris in a circle until they were evenly dispersed around the perimeter, and they opened fire, literally. Flames shot a good fifteen feet from the muzzle of each, and the firefighters walked back and forth, applying the blaze to the rubble.

Suddenly the drywall that had been moving appeared to stand on end. One of the monsters rose from the debris, shrieking painfully. It began walking toward the first firefighter it saw. The man turned the flamethrower on the zombie and hit it full force. Immediately the creature went up in flames, but to everyone's dismay, it kept advancing.

Two of the other firefighters joined the first now. They opened fire with their flamethrowers as well, causing the struggling walking corpse to be engulfed. It continued still, driven by the evil that was inside of it, compelled to eat. Just then a gunshot echoed across the chaos. A bullet hole straight through its head could be seen. It went a few steps then fell to its knees. They kept the flames on full blast, and soon the thing collapsed in a heap on the ground. By the time they took the fire off the monster, it was nothing more than an immobile pile of ashes.

"I couldn't tell if that was one of ours or one of the three that worked there," David said, finally breaking the stunned silence. "Could you?"

Carl shook his head. He couldn't pull his eyes away from the destruction. He wanted to be absolutely positive that another one of those things wasn't going to appear suddenly. "It looked to me like they had one of those restraint jackets on," Carl replied. "It doesn't matter. There were four infected humans that we know of and countless rats in the building."

The men focused their attention more clearly on the debris, now wanting to be sure that critters weren't scurrying out of the mess.

Officer Abana said, "It looks like it is finished to me."

The team of flamethrowers continued to walk the area, dousing the rubble with fire. This went on for the next couple of hours, just to play it safe. Officer Abana turned to David.

"I will need you to fill out a statement for me," he said.

David stated, "The Center for Disease Control will

be taking care of all other formalities, we will need to conduct a thorough inspection of this site before you leave. We need an all-clear."

As the three men stood behind Abana's vehicle, David looked at the destruction. It had been too easy. Something inside him knew this was not it. Something inside him was sure that some of them had somehow gotten out.

He was sure they were a day late and a dollar short.

"Officer Abana," David said, urgently. "I need your help," as if they weren't already spread thin with the situation at hand. "We have a missing Dr. Jonathan Anson."

∞

Captain McElroy had just finished dining on Red, and he was struggling to come back. It seemed that perhaps the captain had eaten a bit too much of his leg, and Red seemed unable to stand. McElroy watched in delight as he struggled, then turned his attention to the metal pole Red had dropped on the floor.

McElroy picked it up in his clumsy hands and looked it over. Then he looked up at the zombies who were still trying to fight their way into the office where the women and children were. He grunted loudly, and taking the pole, barged his way through the crowd of flesh eaters.

He shoved anyone who was in his way aside until he was face to face with the office door. The undead around him grew quiet. The eagerness was evident on all their faces, as they looked to McElroy to help them get inside.

He hit the door hard with a fist, then gave it a firm kick. Women cried out in fear from inside, and this caused the captain to smile. He was almost drooling.

Now that he had gotten a feel for the situation, he took the pole firmly in his hands and rammed it into the door. With the help of a few of the other monsters, they slammed the sharp end of the pole against the handle.

The wood gave way, making a small hole.

Delight spread over McElroy's face. "Again!" They hit the entrance two more times, and it went through the wood.

McElroy got down on one knee and put his face to the gaping hole. There had to be fifteen women and children inside, piled up in a corner crying hysterically.

Now the zombies were actively tearing the entryway apart, and within minutes they were crowding inside. They came down on the group like a festering, poisonous blanket. The women screamed as they fought for the children, but the beasts had their bloody way.

They would have to dock soon, McElroy thought as he chewed on the arm of a kindergartner. There was only a handful left to feast on now. He pushed the thoughts from his mind and enjoyed his meal.

∞

A large team of police officers out of Belize were dressed in safety garb, and they were rifling through the destruction and rubble that had once been Dr. Jonathan Anson's laboratory.

Officer Abana stood away from the wreckage with

the two CDC agents. Once the officers were done rummaging, the agents would step in and conduct a thorough inspection and investigation of the premises. They would then give either the all-clear, or they would have the area evacuated for miles. Only time could tell.

Abana turned to Carl Morgan. "I have never seen such things in my life, Agent Morgan. What has happened here?"

Morgan proceeded to try to explain the situation with the limited knowledge he had, but it all sounded like a bunch of smoke and mirrors. He wasn't interested in making excuses for some sick bastard who wanted to play God. He thought about his words carefully before answering. "This is what happens when a madman tries to exert power that isn't his."

Abana's eyes searched his face, and then he gave an accepting nod. "Yes, madmen. It always goes back to the madmen, does it not?"

The three of them ate an early supper while massive portable lights were set up around the site, and the police continued their tasks. They would all be working well into the night. Both David and Carl were more than ready to put the entire experience behind them. They could only hope that their upcoming investigation would clear them to do so.

When they finished eating and returned to the site, a canopy had been set up where the building used to stand. The place was secure and well lit, and David and Carl were more than anxious to inspect and then put the whole situation behind them.

They worked nearly until midnight and found nothing suspicious. They were able to confirm that the bodies of the individuals, namely Bruce West, Meredith Monroe, Kim Johnson, and Keith Mitchell, were in the building. They all agreed that the body that became animated shortly after the building blew was Dr. Anson himself. But the good news was that none of them were alive. In fact, the bodies were so burned that they crumbled into nothing but ash at the slightest touch, along with all the rats.

They rode back to the police station with Officer Abana and filled out statements and signed stacks of official paperwork, both for Belize and the United States. Then it was time to face the media and answer an endless line of questions about the entire situation. Nothing they told the press jibed with reality. The authorities and government officials had determined from the start that there would be no mention of zombies, monsters, or reanimated bodies.

Instead, they told the press that they had carried out measures to contain a powerful strain of smallpox that had gotten out of the laboratory and begun to spread. They said that while five people had died from the illness, it was now brought under control, and no one in either Belize or any other country needed to worry about it spreading.

It had been successfully eradicated.

Then they all went their separate ways. David Umbridge would stay a few more days to finish up with the local government.

George, Kevin, Rick, and Katy were the only flesh and blood human beings left on the Fantasy Cruise Ship; they were sure of it.

They were still tightly holed up on the bridge, and the entry was still securely barricaded. Even with a crack in the door, it still held. It didn't hurt that the zombies didn't seem to be outside the entrance anymore. For some reason or another, there was nothing but silence in and around the bridge.

All four of them slept soundly for some time, then George woke and began to pace the room. He checked the gauges and knew right away that they would be docking in Houston in two days; it was nearly two in the morning now. He was more than ready to be off this ship, even though he had no idea how he or anyone else would safely get off.

He flattened himself up against the wall near the doorway. He couldn't get to the actual door itself due to all the stuff piled up against it, but he figured he was close enough to it to hear anything that was happening on the other side. He held his breath and listened hard.

It seemed to be dead silent. George thought he heard a loud groaning at one point, but that could have been the wind echoing through something on the ship, he couldn't be sure. He stood there for quite some time listening for something, anything that would tell him whether or not someone was out there watching and waiting.

But the serene silence persisted.

Okay, George thought, they are obviously not out there or they have learned an incredible amount of self-discipline. He didn't believe the latter at all. He knew that those monsters were no more able to be quiet than fly. For some reason or another, they had left the bridge area, at least for the time being.

George looked at the other three people trapped in here with him. Katy was sleeping on the floor like a baby in a fetal position. She had accepted the horror of their situation. She had swallowed all the fear and panic that had threatened to consume her for the last few days. She was convinced they were all going to die, and she knew it was just a matter of time.

Kevin and Rick were another story. Both of them had convinced each other that if they were just given the opportunity, they would single-handedly be able to wipe out the entire zombie population in one fell swoop. When George and Katy asked them for specifics on their plans, they began to stutter and stumble around their words. Finally, they had begun to spout their fantasies only to each other, like a couple of kids.

They all knew full well no one on this boat was going to be able to do anything regarding the living corpses. The best expectation anyone had for escape was to remain hidden and hope to avoid the munchers all together until they were on land, and even then, there was an excellent chance they would become dinner anyway.

Kevin thought about taking the barricades down and leaving the bridge. He was seriously considering taking the risk; after all, what was the worst thing that could happen? Well, he probably wouldn't make it ten feet, and they would start crawling out of the woodwork. He was sure he was faster than they were, the way they loped and lurched, but there were so many of them that all it would take was for them to surround him.

Kevin spoke up, breaking the silence, "let's try the air duct." He was making no sense.

"Brice never came back, Kevin. He is younger and stronger than you, than all of us. I have a feeling we are all that's left." George said, defeated.

No. It was safer to stay right where they were.

The bridge stank horribly of human waste and sweat. They had not eaten or had anything fresh to drink in days, in fact, they had been drinking from a jug of distilled water they found in the emergency bin, but even that was nearly gone.

CHAPTER 20

Carl now stood in the airport, waiting to board his flight. He had checked his bags, obtained his ticket, and checked in with CDC by phone to let them know he was returning home with the samples. Carl was more anxious than he could explain to get out of Belize. If he never returned there again, it would be too soon. After what he had seen, he was ready to cash in on his stockpile of vacation days and put his feet in the sand in Hawaii or something.

"All passengers for Flight 573 to Washington, DC, your flight is ready to board." A small brunette stewardess was standing at a podium waiting to check tickets and get her passengers settled in. Carl got in line, a smile on his face.

The United States had never looked so good.

The local government in Belize was holding an official meeting with one member of the American CDC and a local police officer. They had okayed the destruction of a lab downtown based on information that had been given to them. According to the investigator, the building was crawling with dead things that wouldn't die.

David and Abana sat in the office of the local governor, and they related the story to him, in great detail, of what they had been dealing with. Death and destruction had been unleashed, but the men before him were convinced that they had rectified the situation and had everything under control.

"So tell me," Governor Rodriguez began, "all about the situation, and don't forget to fill me in on how something so unbelievable came to be." He had never heard such far-fetched tales in his life, and if he hadn't gotten the information from trustworthy, professional individuals, he would have never believed a word of it.

David Umbridge spoke first. "Well, sir, we received a report at headquarters in Washington, DC, by email. It was from a laboratory assistant here in Belize by the name of Bruce West. He was assistant to a biologist named Dr. Jonathan Anson."

"It seems he discovered how to 'cheat death,' for lack of a better term."

Rodriguez squinted his eyes. "Cheat death? What do you mean?"

"He created a substance that, when introduced into lab rodents, brought them back to life after death, no matter what condition the body was in. As long as the brain was functional, even minimally, it would reanimate."

Rodriguez listened quietly to the men, trying desperately to put a picture together in his mind of how all this could have taken place. It sounded like some bad fiction, like something one would see only in a movie, but never in real life.

David continued. "The doctor never discovered a way to counteract his findings once they were set in motion. At least, if he did, he never documented it."

David continued. "By the time we were able to get down here, the entire lab was filled with dead animals, and they were all eating each other, then coming back to life. They had killed the secretary and even the assistant himself. Before it was over, we lost two agents to the monsters."

Rodriguez looked over at Officer Abana, disbelief covering his entire face. Abana simply nodded. Yes, everything these men were telling the governor was true. All he could do was validate the information. He was still in a state of shock himself.

"The only way we knew to get the situation under control was to blow up the premises and put fire to everything at the site itself," Umbridge said.

"Sir, we even had one of them try to come towards us after the explosion," Abana said quietly. Rodriguez noted that the policeman was trembling. "I have never seen anything like it."

A secretary entered the office, bearing a small stack of papers. "I will need you all to sign these," Rodriguez said. "They are confidentiality agreements. I do not want the public to hear any of this. It would start a panic that would be hard to control."

The men agreed, and all of them willingly signed.

As Umbridge left the governor's office, he felt relief for the first time. It was over.

Ariana and Brice finally made it to the bridge, and convince George to program the anchor drop one mile from shore. They stood up from the chairs they were sitting in and looked at George. "We're going to try to get to a lifeboat," Brice said simply.

George looked at them like they were nuts. "You're crazy! You'll be killed!" He looked at the others, all of whom were escaping the situation by sleeping. "What about us?"

"Well, you can take a chance and come with us, or you can stay here," he said. "It's up to you."

"So how do you intend to get out of here without putting the rest of us at risk?"

Brice looked up at the grate. "Through there. We'll crawl until we find an exit that is free of these monsters, then we will make our way to the lifeboats by way of the decks."

George was getting irritated. It was like Brice wasn't thinking at all. "You said it yourself. It's a maze of confusion up there." He continued, "If we leave the bridge, the captain will be able to do whatever he wants with this damn boat, and you know what that means! He'll dock it and then go on land. Can you imagine the apocalyptic disaster, Brice?" George continued. "But if we stay here, we're safe, and we can make sure to drop the anchor a safe distance from the port at least then we all have a swimming chance. As far as we know, these savages can't be killed. I'm not willing to take a chance."

Ariana spoke up. "Well, they can be killed; you have

to kill the brain." She paused for a moment, then continued. "I had to kill my mother with a nail file."

"We're going to go," Brice persisted.

George let out an exasperated sigh and shook his head. "I can't leave the ship, regardless of the situation. Sure, our lives are threatened, but like you said, there are people on the mainland we need to think about." He shook his head again. "I'm staying right here and fighting them off as long as I can." George insisted. "You're never going to make it, Stay here."

Ariana shook her head and looked George in the eye. "We are going to warn the authorities."

George could not foresee this plan working for them at all. There was around three-thousand passengers on the ship, and by now, all of them had turned. There wouldn't be any safe place for them to put their feet on the decks.

George finally calmed down and sat in the chair once again.

∞

David sat in his hotel room content; the situation was finally under control. All he had to do was file his final report. He thought about staying in Belize another day to concentrate on his paperwork. David knew if he went home and his wife was there, she would be on him as soon as he walked in, making it impossible to concentrate on his report. As he was straitening up his belongings and condemning himself to another day in Belize, he noticed the backup drives on the desk. It was the surveillance footage of the alleyway. He began to pace the room with his hand on his forehead.

The surveillance footage was eating at his conscience. He desperately needed to have a look; he thought as he snatched one up from the desk and plugged the USB cable into his laptop.

∞

Captain McElroy leaned against an oak desk in one of the offices of the fitness center. He had eaten more than his fill and then watched as the others fought over the few scraps that remained after the women and children turned. Now it was nearly silent in the center, and the only audible sounds were coming from two of the zombies, who were trying to eat each other.

Awkwardly, McElroy maneuvered his heavy, if not rotting, frame, standing as straight as he could. He struggled to guide his own body out to where the two were battling if you could call it that, then he drew back his leg and gave a clumsy kick to the one nearest him.

"Get up and find others," McElroy spat. "We have little time to get the job done on board. Find others!"

They scrambled on their hands and knees, separating from each other. Both had mouthfuls they were chewing on, but their fear of McElroy took precedence. They crawled away from his swinging foot as quickly as possible, disappearing from his sight.

He turned around and staggered a bit, catching himself just in time to keep from toppling over. He took a ragged breath and tried to focus his one good eye. That was when he heard the whimpering.

McElroy stopped suddenly and began to sniff the

air. He could hear the sobs, but could not tell by sound where they were coming from. He raised his nose high in the air and inhaled deeply.

It was coming from his left.

He turned sharply, nearly falling over in the process. It was coming from the closed door, the entry which Red came out of when he first arrived at the fitness center.

The crying was very distinct; McElroy knew someone was in there before he even pressed his dead ear against the door. He listened just for the pleasure of it, then laughed a deep, loud, guttural laugh. The crying stopped immediately. Whoever it was heard him laugh, and this made him chuckle even louder.

Now he hit the door hard with his left fist and ran his tongue up and down the wood. He could smell the man inside so clearly that he could almost taste him. What an ideal way to top off such a fulfilling meal than with a whining, crying boy for dessert?

"Hello?" the man said from the other side of the door. "Big Red, is that you?"

McElroy stroked the door with the palms of his hands. "Yes….," he said. "Let me in. They're after me…"

The voice was closer now. "It is really you?"

The door handle jiggled. "Yes," McElroy growled in a low tone. "Me."

McElroy heard things being shuffled around inside, boxes, and other items being flung away from the door. Suddenly all the activity stopped. The man on the other side said once more, "Who is it again? I can't tell by your voice."

"Me," the captain repeated his voice a bit clearer this time.

The man unlocked the door and opened it a crack. That was all McElroy needed. He came at Tom with all the weight of his body, and as quickly as possible. He tackled the man to the floor, both of them landing in a heap, and then he bit into Tom's inner calf.

They fought and struggled violently, but the man was no match for the big, tough, putrid sea captain. In no time at all, he was pinned down, and he was an entrée. He lay in submission, being eaten as his left leg jerked, and his right eye twitched open and closed.

The wet smacking sound of McElroy having his way with Tom filled the entire fitness center.

∞

The balcony door was open, and the wind blew the curtain in towards David as he sat nervously at the desk in his hotel room. His eyes were wide, while he watched the footage playing on his computer. His stomach sank the instant he saw two tourists enter the mouth of the alley. As the two were approaching the dog, David lifted his head up in an over-exhausted motion. He exhaled a deep breath, and he muttered the word, "Fuck!" He inhaled and returned his eyes to the screen, sitting up in his chair. He could plainly see the boy's hand get nipped, and he watched as the boy instantly pulled away from the pup and put the wound to his mouth. David thought to himself. There was no other reason for those movements unless the boy was bitten, especially followed by the jerking motion he just witnessed. That solidified the containment breach. He knew full well the boy was exposed. This case just took a massive turn for the worst. In all his career, David could have never imagined such an event, yet here it was unfolding before his very eyes. He was waist-deep in a possible pandemic of mass proportions.

David was pacing in his hotel room, the phone receiver on his ear. The phone rang and rang as David watch the curtains blow in from the open balcony. "Officer Abana Its David Umbridge. Sorry to call you so late, but I need your help."

First thing in the morning, the two men met at the store next to Anson's lab. After obtaining the charge receipts, they deduced who the parents were of the two kids in the alley. Shortly after and some tedious legwork, David was on the phone with Ray once again. I believe our zombie situation is not over."

"Look, you're not putting zombies on this report. If I hear the word zombies one more time, I'm going to recommend to the board for early retirement. Is that clear!" He exclaimed in a matter of fact tone. "Maybe you should take some time off after this assignment regardless?" his supervisor questioned. "I'm sure there is a logical explanation." Ray threatened in a forceful tone.

"I believe the two kids in the alley are passengers aboard the Fantasy Lines cruise ship. Judging by its itinerary, it's scheduled to dock in Cozumel Mexico tomorrow. I will get ahold of the port authority to inform them of the situation and quarantine the ship." David said as he informed Ray before he ended the phone call.

On the way to the airport to catch his flight to Mexico, David made a few calls. After talking to the port in Cozumel, he dialed the Coast Guard.

"US Coast Guard agent Mel speaking."

"Good morning, agent. My name is David Umbridge from the CDC. I believe with your equipment. You could locate a missing ship at sea?" David spent a few minutes explaining to the agent there was a family on board that had vital information to an investigation he was working on. It was imperative and in the best interest for the safety and security of the United States that he contact the family onboard.

"We have a small vessel on maneuvers in the gulf I will have them check for your lost cruise ship." The agent replied as they disconnected the call.

CHAPTER 21

The Coast Guard vessel was cutting through the water at a high rate of speed. The lieutenant's voice broke the silence on the bridge. "The missing Fantasy Lines cruise ship we are looking for should be headed to Cozumel. Unfortunately, everything in the area is accounted for, commander."

"Widen the search area." The commander exclaimed.

Within a few minutes, the silence was broken once again. "Con radar, I have an unidentified contact baring 342, that could be a ship, sir."

The commander instantly barked the orders. "Make normal one-third turn's, all ahead full set course 342, let's try to get a definitive classification."

∞

Captain McElroy was looking out to sea with a concerned look on his face. He turned to his officers, "I see a ship in the distance; it looks to be the meddling coastguard." The captain grunted as he chewed on what appeared to be a toddler's forearm. "Signal it with lights and load a dinghy with a small army." He barked to his minions. "Fresh meat!"

"Con radar contact steady at 1200 yards and closing, sir."

"Continue course and speed," the orders echoing in the bridge.

"Commander," the lieutenant approached and stood at attention, "the cruise ship is signaling SOS distress, and it appears they are currently lowering a lifeboat to us full of passengers. We have tried to hail the ship with no response, Commander."

"All hands on deck, prepare for medical transport."

The announcement echoed throughout the small ship, and semen scurried about in preparation to take on the injured passengers. Within minutes the Coast Guard was overrun. Bullets sprayed everywhere, unfortunately hitting a fuel tank that set off a chain reaction. The fire made its way to the storage tanks igniting thousands of gallons of diesel fuel. The massive explosion shook the cruise ship causing everyone on board to fall to their knees. The sound of breaking glass rang through the cruise liner; the smell of diesel fuel was overpowering.

McElroy was watching the action from above. He stood at the railing with a smile picking his teeth with a woman's manicured finger. Rubble and fragments of the Coast Guard's vessel showered down on the luxury liner. Leaving nothing but a shell as it took on water. Pleased with the destruction and chuckling grotesquely, McElroy patiently witnessed the Coast Guard's vessel descend into the deep.

Ariana and Brice winced in pain as the explosion echoed through the ductwork, shaking them off their knees'. They were choking and coughing from the smell of burning diesel fuel; they braced to steady themselves from the ship rocking.

"What the hell was that?" Ariana exclaimed.

"I'm not sure. I wonder if it came from the bridge?" He thought quietly, could McElroy be smart enough to rig a bomb? Perhaps someone took out the engines? Multiple scenarios were playing out in his mind.

Ariana finally snapped him out of his reverie, "We need to get off this thing; let's get moving." She said as she put her shirt over her mouth in an attempt to filter some of the smoke. "Come on, follow me."

Ariana took the lead confident enough she could find them a way out.

∞

All of the zombies, except for Captain McElroy, were wandering the ship aimlessly. They staggered around, moaning and groaning, and they were starved. They had left the bridge alone, just as the captain had directed, and it had been easy when they discovered the group of people in the gym. But now all of them set their thoughts back on the fresh meat on the bridge. They were all starting to shuffle back in that direction slowly.

The captain, of course, was in the lead, with the central focus being the door to the bridge. Their hunger was making them even more temperamental, and they were beginning to fight with each other. They were also making second-hand meals out of the weak.

McElroy could have cared less. His focus was back on the bridge now, and he was determined to get inside and have his feast before he took back control of the bridge. This time the captain had brought a fire ax with him, and he led the masses. Yes, he would be inside the bridge in no time at all.

Katy sat in the same spot on the bridge that she had been sitting in for an eternity now. Her knees were drawn up under her chin, and her arms were wrapped around her legs to hold them in place. She seemed to think somewhere in the back of her mind that the smaller she could make herself, the less of a chance there was that the monsters would notice her when they finally got in.

Katy glanced out of the corner of her eye at the deck officer. His eyes looked vacant as if he no longer resided within the shell that resembled Kevin. He had dark bags under his eyes, and they stood out in dark contrast against his pasty white skin. Katy scanned the room and set her sights on George; he had his ear up against the wall just underneath the air duct. He was paying no mind to anything or anyone around him.

She scanned the room again. Where was Rick? She panicked a bit, and her eyes scanned much more rapidly, but he was nowhere to be seen. Did he die? Did he just 'disappear'? She began to whimper to herself, which managed to capture George's attention.

He turned his head sharply and focused his eyes on her as best he could in the dim light. "Are you okay, Katy?"

"Where is Rick?" Katy asked softly.

A shadow crossed over George's face as he climbed off the chair. He put a finger to his lips as if to tell her to keep it down, and then he sank to the floor by her side.

A voice came out of the shadows. "I'm right here."

It was Rick. He had completely isolated himself from the others during this ordeal; George had nearly forgotten he existed.

George knew what that meant. It meant he was the only one left on the bridge with the knowledge and experience to get them out of this alive. It was not a responsibility he wanted to have.

A sharp, splintering noise suddenly came from the door. It sounded as if the half dead's that had been so persistent were finally making way. George quickly stood to his feet.

"Rick, Kevin, I need your help to pile the rest of this stuff in front of the door." He stopped to check the gauges; they were still on course. All he wanted was to drop anchor as close as possible. George resigned himself, at that very moment, to the fact that he would not be getting off this ship alive. He went over to the cabinet, which held the flares and a flare gun. He opened it and removed two flares and the weapon itself.

He and the other two put every loose thing they could find up against the door. It was actually reinforced quite well. Zombies were throwing their bodies against the door and pounding and clawing. But nothing that was part of the barricade moved even a fraction of an inch. He knew they still had a bit of time.

Katy was crying quietly to herself in her spot, her head buried in her arms, which rested on her knees. George bent down and put an arm around her shoulders. "We are safe for now, Katy. Try to relax." She didn't acknowledge him, and she didn't stop crying. He stood, knowing it was best to leave her to herself.

George turned to the men. "When we anchor, If we can survive until then, we have a chance, but we really have to pull together to accomplish that." The men looked at him and offered him a single nod, each as confirmation. He knew that no one in that room believed they were going to make it.

They listened to the animalistic sounds coming from outside the bridge door and tried to keep as calm as they could.

∞

Katy was sound asleep, and stuck in a nightmare.

The monsters were coming into the bridge. They had successfully beaten their way through both the door and the barricade, and in her dream, she was huddled in a shadow in the corner, watching them devour her three companions. They ripped at flesh and broke bones, but it didn't matter. Her shipmates were coming back to life, bigger and better than ever.

In her dream, Katy began to scream.

Suddenly, she was jerked away violently. It was

Kevin, and he was aggressively shaking her.

"Katy, you have to wake up!" She looked at him, confused, and tried to separate the pieces of reality from the pictures she saw in her slumber.

Then she heard the noise. It was a loud hacking sound, and it came one after another after another.

"Wha-What is that?" She tried to scoot away from Kevin, but she was up against the wall.

Kevin grabbed her arm and pulled her to her feet. "It's them. They are breaking down the door with some kind of weapon. We have to get in the ventilation shaft and try to get out of here."

She looked up to see Rick's legs dangling out; he was already half-way in. She didn't argue with Kevin. She waited for Rick to get all the way inside the duct, then she got on the chair and gave him her hands. He pulled, and Kevin pushed, and together they hoisted her up into the vent with no problem at all.

Another loud crack came from the door. Some of the items they used to barricade it toppled from the top of the pile to the ground. Kevin looked petrified.

"Help me up fast!" Katy moved aside, George and Rick grabbed Kevin's arms and began to pull.

Now the monsters were throwing themselves at the door violently. Each time they made contact with it, more of the barricade came apart. "Hurry," Kevin was saying in a panicked voice, "They are almost through!"

George and Rick tried to pull, but the stout Kevin was so damn heavy. "Kevin, we can't do it. You've got to get more height!"

Kevin let go of Rick's arms and got down from the chair. He looked around the room, and his eyes settled on the bucket they had all been using for a toilet. It would have to do.

Holding his breath, he stood to the side of the chair and turned the bucket upside down. Feces and urine spilled onto the chair, and all over the floor, now was not the time to get squeamish. He stepped in some of the mess as he climbed on top of the bucket. The zombies were through the door, and they were violently working their way through the items in the barricade.

Kevin started to panic. Rick and George had him by the arms once again, pulling as hard as they could. Kevin's feet were no longer touching the bucket. Instead, his legs dangled as he tried to pull himself up.

Now their growls and moans were thunderous. They were making their way onto the bridge, and a couple of them were standing at Kevin's feet, arms in the air, grabbing at his dangling legs. He felt his pants falling as one of them got a firm grip on his legs and began to pull him down.

"They've got me, Rick," he panted, his eyes wide with fear and the reality of the situation. "Help me!"

"We're trying Kevin. You've got to pull yourself up. You have to help us more."

Katy was behind them, tears streaming down her face. She desperately wanted to help Rick and George pull, but there was no room for her. They were able to get him into the duct up to his chest.

"We've got you," Rick said, straining to pull him in

further, but suddenly he was jerked backward. His eyes filled with terror and pain.

As soon as George, Rick, and Katy realized life had left his eyes, they released his arms. He fell down and out of sight in a split second. "Go, go, go!" George was yelling.

Rick turned to Katy and said in a stern voice, "Let's go!"

The three started to crawl aimlessly through the air ducts, but Rick knew it was futile. As soon as the monsters were done with Kevin, they would get into the ductwork themselves, and then he, Katy, and George would be as good as dead.

They pushed the thoughts out of their minds and began to crawl like mad through the air shaft.

"We need to split up," George said, take the first turn. "Get her to safety I will lure them this way."

Captain McElroy was on the bridge standing at the control panel and checking out the route they were on. The fools had programmed the autopilot to drop anchor. If they had been successful, it would have flubbed up the captain's plans somewhat. All looked well now, and they were good to go and dock. He knew his way around Houston; anywhere else would have bred confusion in his decaying mind.

He looked up just as the zombies were pulling Kevin Hines out of the duct for good. He smiled, and a single tooth dropped from his gums. It was time for a fresh bite to eat. The others were already all over the guy. The captain had to kick a few of his minions aside just to get close enough to dine. They didn't have much time to eat, however. Kevin began to reanimate almost immediately.

The rotters were narrowing things down now.

As Kevin's body struggled to adjust to being dead, the captain looked up at the air duct and the opening that led to it. How many had managed to get through there before they made their way on the bridge? One, as he had seen, or were there more than that tunneling through the ducts, trying to save their own pointless lives.

He walked over to the stool-covered chair that was placed strategically beneath the opening. He paid no mind to the feces that was getting all over him as he climbed onto the chair and bucket. Once he was up, he struggled to maintain his balance, hanging on to the opening as if for dear life. He peered into the duct.

Captain McElroy could see no one, but he could hear them, and he could most certainly smell them. Yes, three different scents were coming from the vent. Three living beings had escaped through here, each one alive, and each one fresh for the picking.

He tried to hoist himself into the duct, but lack of control over his own body did not let him do it. He fell off the chair hard, landing on his back right on top of a group of wandering souls that were standing below him.

"Help me, you worthless bums!" he snarled at them, and they complied immediately. The captain climbed back on top of the bucket. He pulled at the duct with his arms while the zombies pushed at his legs and rear end.

In under a minute, he was inside the air shaft and crawling with a vengeance.

There were three ways to go. McElroy looked in each direction, and then took a giant whiff of each tunnel. One of them had gone straight ahead, while the other two had taken the vent to the right.

George screamed, "This way, you filthy animal!" in an attempt to lure him away from the other two.

"George, I will be back for you!" McElroy spat his voice echoing grotesquely.

The captain had always said two were better than one. He took a right and began to crawl forward to his next meal.

R.W.K. Clark

CHAPTER 22

David arrived in Cozumel, expectantly waiting for the cruise ship to arrive. "What is this I hear about you blowing up a building in Belize? Now I find out you're in Cozumel, are you out of your mind?" Clarissa Thompson was furious with David.

"I believe the Fantasy Lines Cruise ship is carrying a small child that could have been bitten by an infected dog. It's docking today. I plan on quarantining the ship here in Cozumel." David said, "look, could I speak to Ray, please?"

"I already told you he is out of the office." Clarissa snapped as they ended the call.

∞

Katy and Rick were crawling aimlessly through the ducts; neither of them had any idea which direction they were heading. All they knew was that they were still alive, and they wanted to stay that way. That meant they had to press on.

They would stop and look through every grate they had encountered. Finally, there were no zombies to be seen. "Where do you think they are?" Katy asked.

"They're on the bridge," Rick replied. "Soon

enough, they will get in the duct and start looking for us. They will know we came in here."

Katy gave a whimper, so Rick took her hand and pulled her, letting her know she had to keep moving. "There will be plenty of time for crying when we get out of this mess, girl. Focus, for now, cry later."

She wiped her eyes with the back of her hand and kept crawling. She had to be brave, but she knew her courage was ready to crumble at any second. It was so hard to keep your ears and eyes peeled while you tried to gain ground.

They took a right, a left, another left, and then another right. Katy had lost all sense of direction at the first turn, and while Rick was better in that department, he still felt strangely lost and out of touch with his surroundings. He made it a point to stop and peer through each grate in an effort to get a handle on where exactly they were on the ship. From what he could see, they were at the opposite end of the vessel from the lifeboats, and those small watercrafts were their only hope.

They stopped for a moment and rested. Katy turned to Rick, her eyes shadowed and confused. "What do you think happened to George?"

Rick looked into Katy's eyes. She sounded like a small child that was lost at the mall and couldn't find her mother. The girl was attractive, with soft blonde hair and blue eyes. In any other situation, he would have made it a point to ask her out, but after watching each other defecate in a bucket for days, well, it sort of changed things.

"I don't know, Katy," he replied simply.

"They're going to follow us, you know," she said.

Rick nodded pointlessly in the darkness. "I know."

After a bit, he tugged on her arm. "Are you ready to set out again?"

"As ready as I will ever be," she replied.

They set off on their hands and knees once again, and they crawled until they reached a 'y'-shaped junction. Rick turned to Katy and smiled. "Left or right?"

She gave a weak smile in return. "Eany, meany, miney, moe," she said.

Rick chuckled. At least she was in reasonably good spirits, and she wasn't hysterical.

Suddenly, they heard a noise from the direction they had come. It wasn't just any noise. It was the sound of dragging like whoever was crawling was having to pull a gimp leg along or something. Katy covered her mouth with her hands and looked at Rick with fear-stricken eyes. He put a finger over his lips to let her know to keep still. They listened closely.

Someone was humming the sing-song tune, "Yo Ho Ho and a Bottle of Rum." It was macabre and terrifying. Rick pulled on Katy's hand. "We have to get moving now, fast honey," he told her.

They began to crawl like mad, not caring if they made noise or not. They knew as well as the zombies that they were likely the only living beings left on the ship. The monsters knew they were in here, and one of them was certainly on their tail. Rick was willing to bet it was the captain himself, if not more.

They went to the right at the 'y,' then took another right, then a left. The next vent they came to was directly over the deck by the pool. Rick turned to Katy. "Move back a bit. I'm going to kick the grille free."

Katy did as she was told, and Rick lay down on his back. Using both feet, he kicked hard at the panel, but only ended up denting it severely. Rick paid no mind to his failure, though. He only kept kicking.

After about the fourth kick, the screws and grate ripped away from the ceiling. The vent fell to the deck below with a loud 'clang!' He turned and looked at his companion. "There are going to be cannibals down there, but we will die up here for sure. The captain is on our tail."

Katy only nodded at him. Nothing really mattered to her anymore. She knew full well they weren't going to make it out of this mess alive.

Rick dropped down to the deck from the duct, landing solidly on his feet. He looked up at Katy and lifted his arms. "Jump, Katy. I'll catch you, I promise. Don't be afraid."

She dangled her legs out of the opening and said, "I'm not afraid. Are you ready?"

Suddenly a wet, raspy voice came from behind her. "I am more than ready."

She turned to see the captain upon her. The skin of his right cheek was sloughing off and lying partially on his jaw. She could see the dark gap of his eye socket around his eye, and his breath smelled like rotting food.

Katy screamed, and the last thing Rick saw was her tiny body being jerked back into the duct violently.

"Katy!" he screamed, but all he got in response was the sound of chewing and ripping. Rick took off running across the deck.

He didn't have time to care. He had to make his way back to the other side of the ship. He had to make his way to the lifeboats.

The air was cold, and it was dark, George sat looking at the sliver of light reflecting off the ductwork from the vent opening. Since being forced off the bridge, he knew McElroy would now be able to dock the ship. Surely the Captain would alter the anchor drop. He needed a plan B, and he needed it now.

Mutiny was at hand. McElroy's actions were nothing less than a criminal conspiracy to overthrow the human race. Finally, George came to the conclusion the only way to stop the cruise liner was to manually stop the ship all together. On a suicide mission to stop an apocalypse, he headed to the fuel storage, his plan to ignite the diesel fuel with a flare and save humanity. As second in command, he felt it was now his duty to go down with the ship.

∞

There comes Phu-fa-lou trotting, ravenous like never before. Sporting black eyes in stark contrast against her blood-soaked white fur. The adorable pup now a deranged Pomeranian with an appetite for brains. Growling, snarling and foaming at the mouth as she hopped up into the arms of McElroy. The captain's maniacal laugh was filling the air.

Captain McElroy stood on the deck. All the zombies on the ship, numbering more than three-thousand, were gathered, and he was able to look up and address them all clearly.

"We will dock in only a few hours, and then we will be free. Prepare yourselves," McElroy told them all, as he stroked the puppy in his arms, "for they are going to put up a heck of a fight."

He was met with groans that were meant to be cheers, and screams of agreement. There was no more meat on the ship. It was time for him to make his way back to the bridge and bring this big boat home. There would be a bit of confusion since he had destroyed the radio early on, but he knew he would be able to get approval to dock.

Soon he and the rest of them would be able to spread their wings on dry ground.

∞

Ariana stopped crawling and turned to Brice, "I smell food." Neither of them had eaten in what seemed like days. They slowly approached the vent and looked out to see a small kitchen area. The smell of pastries and coffee filled the air.

"I know this café," finally a familiar location. "We need to get our energy up," Brice said as he quietly and desperately undid the screws of the grille.

Within moments the two of them were eating cold cuts and drinking water like they haven't seen it in weeks. Ariana stood at the coffee machine, lifting a pot that had obviously been on the warmer for days. She took a whiff and scrunched her nose. "Yeah, that's disgusting," she said as she flipped the switch off.

Just then, the door swung open, and zombies' swarmed in like fly's on a picnic. Gunshots rang out as Ariana made precision headshots one after another. Brice was shocked and very impressed by Ariana's quick response. Her marksmanship was second to none. He just watched as she went from clip to clip, till the horde subsided. Swiftly she stepped over the bodies piled up at her feet and peered outside the door.

"What do you see," Brice asked?

"Looks like we rang the dinner bell. Quick, give me something to wedge the door closed." She blurted while turning her back and leaning against the door. Within seconds they had the room secure and were making their way into the ductwork.

As Brice boosted Ariana back into the air shaft, he worked out the path they would take to the lifeboats in his mind.

R.W.K. Clark

CHAPTER 23

David was on the phone with the Coastguard. "Agent Mel this is David Umbridge, I'm following up on my lost cruise ship."

"Mr. Umbridge, we have lost contact with one of our own Coast Guard vessels while on assignment. I'm sorry we haven't found your missing cruise ship, there will be a delay until we can get another ship in the area. Until then, I'm afraid we won't be able to continue the search." Agent Mel was saying.

Picking up on this detail, David questioned the agent, "Agent, what was the location of your vessel when you lost contact?"

"Approximately 150 nautical miles off the coast of Galveston Island. We had an explosion on board. That is all I can disclose." The agent said as they disconnected the call.

David thought to himself it's obvious the ship skipped docking in Cozumel and was almost to the Houston port. All eyes were on the sinking coast guard vessel, and no eyes on the cruise liner headed for land.

∞

George was hiding in a crawl space under the lowest

deck. He had been there for the last several hours, and his limbs were completely asleep. He was only a couple hundred yards from the propulsion systems, but just as he had recognized that fact, he was confronted by several hungry monsters. George had made his way here and concealed himself in the space that was used by maintenance.

So far, so good.

He was getting ready to make a run for it. All he needed to do was make it that short three-hundred feet, just a hop, a skip, and jump, and he would basically be home free. He listened carefully for any sound coming from the deck above, but he heard nothing.

George lifted up on the panel over his head very slowly. He raised it only about a half an inch, and he let his eyes skim the area as best as he could. From what little George could see, there was no one on the deck at all. He lifted the panel even further.

Now he was able to stick his head up a bit. He did a complete 360, and when he was satisfied that no one was observing him, he removed the panel all the way and hoisted himself out of the crawl space. He looked all around him, his heart pounding violently in his chest. Now was his chance to go for it.

He took off sprinting in the direction of the engine room. The whole time he ran, he looked around him, but none of the monsters could be seen or heard. Where were they all, he wondered to himself? He had no idea how many real humans were left on board, trying to save their own lives. His stomach lurched violently at the thought. George ran up a narrow corridor that had at one time led to crew cabins. It too, was empty. At the end, he took a sharp left, then a right, and then he was at the watertight mechanical room entry. He bent over and put his hands on his knees, his breathing ragged. He had to catch his breath. With one hand on the flair gun and one had on the hydraulic lever, he was ready to enter the engine control room. The door clanged and creaked as it opened, the beeping noise from the door warning echoed through the hallway. Just a few feet in front of him were the large fire doors. As he stepped into the room and without warning, he was covered in animated corpses. The chief engineer himself sank his teeth into George's neck, blood squirting out profusely. George crumpled to his knees as he squeezed the trigger of the flare gun, sparks flew, and the bright ball of fire ricocheted around the area. The smell and acrid air from the burning flare filled the room. Instantly the fire suppression system came on in full force. George laid hopelessly on the floor, his leg twitching as he was being devoured.

∞

"It seems to me the zombies evolve and become more sentient as they inhabit their human body." Brice was saying as he and Ariana crawled to the next opening and looked out.

"I agree with the way my mother talked to me. She seemed strategic and dangerous. I couldn't imagine what would happen if they reach land. Could they evolve and eventually blend in with the general population?" Ariana was horrified at the thought.

Brice recognized the deck below immediately, stacks of life preservers were neatly placed along the deck wall. He sucked in his breath. The lifeboats were on the other side! He knew where he was now, and his confidence level took a boost. In no time, he found himself looking down on the first of many lifeboats they had made it.

He stopped and listened carefully, but he could hear nothing. He then reached in his pocket and took out a pair of pliers. He got hold of the screw and proceeded to reverse it out of the hole.

After a moment, the screw fell out onto the deck below. It made a sound that seemed to be terribly loud to Brice, and he froze. Ariana was on alert and terrified. The two listened for a moment but couldn't hear anything.

He did the other screws, each of them falling out one at a time. The last one hit the floor rolling into the drain, making excessive noise. By holding on to the panel, he was able to hold it steady, push it free, and pull it silently into the air duct with them.

"We're as good as out of here," he whispered to Ari. "The first occupied land we see, we'll stop and get help."

He let his feet fall down through the hole, first and slowly lowered his body. He would come down on the deck, followed by Ariana, then all they had to do was climb over the railing. The lifeboat was secured right there.

His feet hit the deck. He couldn't believe that they

made it. He quietly helped Ariana down to the floor.

"You're just in time," a raspy voice said from behind him.

In a flash, Brice turned around. He barely got a look at the group of rotting cannibals, of which there were about five. I couldn't hear them, he thought to himself, and they were on him.

The two opened fire on the zombies, taking them out systematically as they ran to find shelter. They rounded the corner.

"No!" Ari screamed as a rotting cadaver bit down on Brice's neck. Brice could feel his flesh ripping and was aware of the warm blood pouring over his neck. His mind knew what was happening while his body stayed in denial; he felt no pain.

Two shots rang out, with a swift double-tap of the trigger. The animal's head snapped back, and the body crumpled to the deck. Ari dropped the gun and grabbed Brice to comfort him. She held her first love tightly, gently giving him one last kiss.

Suddenly Brice's milky white eyes fluttered open. The eyes that once held her gaze were now opaque, empty and cold. The Brice she knew was no longer there, and it was at that moment she knew what she had to do. With shooting pain in her stomach and an ache in her heart, she put the gun to his temple and pulled the trigger. "I give you mercy," she whispered.

Just then, a horde of zombies rounded the corner, giving her no time to mourn her loss. She snapped into action once again.

Ariana turned the corner in full force heading for the lifeboats. With a hoard of supernaturals at her heels, and her options growing thin, she dropped to the deck in a roll. Her confidence level off the charts, the once sweet and timid animal lover, was now a mature badass warrior. Landing upright on her feet, she came out of a tuck and roll guns blazing mowing down the hoard with a full clip. After a moment, she stood up straight and went to the railing. There on the other side was a lifeboat, secured and waiting for her to free it so it could take her to safety. She climbed the railing and dropped into the vessel feet first. She was on the boat.

She reached into her pocket and removed Brice's penknife. Once it was open, she began to saw through the ropes that secured the lifeboat. Her heart pounded so hard she could have sworn that anyone within a hundred feet could hear it, and she tried to will it to calm down.

She was almost through the final rope when she happened to glance up. There stood two half-rotten freak shows. They were leaning over the railing, swinging their arms and hands in an attempt to reach her. Fortunately, she was out of their grasp.

She began to saw feverishly at the rope. One of the zombies was trying to scale the railing. He had one leg over and was struggling to swing the second one over as well. The other muncher was snarling and smacking his lips. Drool ran from them and hit her in the face.

Rapidly the final rope gave, and with a hard jolt, the lifeboat broke free from its position. Ariana's stomach went into her throat as the boat swiftly fell, and she nearly bounced out completely when it hit the water. Cool brine mist the air as the lifeboat hit the ocean in a splash, walkers raining down upon her. She shook her head to clear it. She was free; she was on the water.

Within seconds, the undead were climbing down the ropes and falling to the sea around her. Some were falling from the ship landing flat on the lifeboat. Fear and anger coursing through her veins as she kicked them from the craft in a flash.

Sharks were swarming the lifeboat within seconds in a feeding frenzy, blood-red seas surrounding her.

She screamed at the top of her lungs, "Yeah, c'mon out here!" watching the beasts on the ship as they swung their arms and growled and moaned.

Panic struck; she removed the straps holding the flat blade oars. Ariana got the paddles that were attached to the inner walls of the lifeboat. She knew the direction she needed to go, and she set off with vigor rowing for her dear life to getaway.

Thoughts of Brice were clouding her concentration as Ariana franticly rowed the dinghy to increase the gap from the ship. She fully intended to reach land before the cruise liner did, so she could warn the authorities to stop this madness, this horrid nightmare. Ari continued to paddle, and the distance between the lifeboat and the cruise ship grew larger and larger. Soon she could no longer hear their growls or the chaos of those on the boat searching for their next meal. Ariana was safe, and she was on her way to Galveston Island.

The sound of the ship growing faint in the distance. For the first time in days, Ariana was able to enjoy a deep breath. A tear ran down her cheek as she had to relive the horror in her mind. Unexpectedly, without warning, a misty chill hit her skin as water sprayed her from the side. In the corner of her eye, all she could see was a glimpse of pointy white teeth that snapped within inches of her face. In a flash she opened fire, aiming at the shark, she hit it dead square in the head, gunshots rang out across the sea. The faint sound of gunfire echoing off the hull of the massive cruise liner. Finally, feeling a sense of relief, Ariana watched as its lifeless body slipped back into the blood-red sea.

CHAPTER 24

Rick Harris was officially the only living human being left on the Fantasy Cruise Ship.

He was squatting down in an empty maintenance closet, spraying air freshener from a can every five minutes to cover his scent. He wasn't feeling very positive about his chances of survival. Something told him this was going to be his final cruise.

His mind was wandering, and he was losing the will to fight. He tried to listen for the sounds of the monsters, but now they were beginning to sound like everything else; they were starting to sound 'normal.' Even Rick knew what that meant. It meant he was on his last leg, that he was running out of steam.

Regardless, he knew that he couldn't simply continue to hide in here; they were going to find him, air freshener or not. Every now and then, he thought he could hear one or more of them shuffling past the closet door. He found he felt more and more tempted each time just to open the closet door and say, 'Here I am!'' He couldn't even bolster his courage enough to do that.

Rick pulled a pocketknife his father had given him

from his slacks and looked at it in the dim light. It had three different blades, a screwdriver, and a pair of scissors.

Now it was all he had that stood between life and death. He opened the largest blade and let the dim light bounce off of the silver edge playfully. It made him smile.

Rick shifted his weight and adjusted his position. His legs were falling asleep from squatting.

He decided to come out of that closet swinging. He was going to fight them to the death, even though he knew that death was going to be his own. He would rather surrender on his terms than have them capture him against his will. It was the only way he could see that would allow him to maintain any semblance of control.

His mind flashed back to when he got hired by the cruise line. He had been so excited. The pay was outstanding, the benefits incomparable, and he was guaranteed a party basically every night of his life. It was a young twenty-something's dream job.

How naïve he had been after all these years! Nothing in life came without strings attached. He had been blind and greedy. He had been downright stupid.

He stood and shook his legs out one by one, bringing the blood flow back into them. As the tingling subsided, he considered his next move. The next time he heard one of those creatures outside the door, he was going to charge it and drive his knife through its eyeball. Then he was going to fight them with all he had until his life ended, and he was sure it would end.

But he would go down battling hard.

He pressed his ear against the maintenance closet door and listened. He chose to be patient and continued to listen. He wanted more than one to be out there. He wanted it to end fast. It would take two or three of them for that to happen.

That was when he heard it: the grunting and moaning and growling that only the monsters did. He listened closer until he was sure. Yes, there were several of them near the closet. It was time to man up and face the facts.

Rick Harris steadied his grip on the pocket knife and swung the maintenance closet door open with all his might. He flew out of the closet, screaming like Rambo and swinging the blade all around. There in front of him stood Jason and Adam first, they just looked at Rick, confused, and trying to figure out what was happening.

But it didn't take long for the facts to register in what little they had left of their minds, and they began to lurch and stagger toward him. He continued to swing, hollering at the top of his lungs. "Come and get me! Come and get a piece of this!"

He began to high kick and whip around like a master of karate, though he knew nothing of the art. He was only able to do this silliness for a brief moment, then the father-son duo were on him. He slashed at them and stabbed at them but with minimal effect.

They slammed him to the floor, and he struggled against them as they knelt next to him and began to enjoy their next meal. He registered the biting and the ripping, but he felt no pain. As a matter of fact, he started laughing hysterically.

"Yeah, you have it," he screamed. "All of this is for you."

Right then, Jason ripped his jugular out with his teeth, and Rick bled out in less than a minute and a half. The scene before his eyes faded to black, and the sounds he had once heard became silent.

Now he could finally put this all behind him.

∞

David was scrambling through the airport, running to board his flight. He made numerous phone calls one after another, desperately trying to address the situation at hand. Once again, he held the cell tightly against his ear as it rang. A snotty voice finally answered the call. "Hello, Houston port authority how may I help you?"

"This is David Umbridge from the CDC. I'm trying to locate a Fantasy Lines Cruise ship, I believe, is headed to the port."

"Let me check," after a brief pause, the snobbish voice continued. "Yes, that ship is due back in 3 days."

"I have reason to believe it is carrying a zombie virus onboard, and we need to quarantine it," David said blatantly.

The operator nit his brow, 'zombies,' he thought to himself this guy sounds like a wackjob. "Okay, we will do that," he exclaimed. He agreed with everything David said just to appease him until he hung up the receiver. He laughed as he collected his things to prepare for a shift change, deliberately disregarding the warning David tried to convey.

Content the call went well, David clicked his seatbelt and fastened it tightly aboard the flight to Houston international.

R.W.K. Clark

CHAPTER 25

Ariana sat in the lifeboat, paddling furiously and looking over her shoulder. Well over two hours had passed, and she could see the ship behind her, but just barely. It was making headway, but she was ahead of the game.

She could see the busy bay up ahead, and while she wasn't quite close enough to make out the people milling around, she could hear the echoes of the full day they all were having. The sound of them yelling at each other, occasional loud laughter, and the like. With each passing second, she grew closer and closer, and it motivated her to paddle harder, harder, even harder.

She was exhausted, dehydrated, and panic struck. Her mind turned to Brice. She wondered what happened to her dad. Was he still holding off the monsters? Was he still holed up safely on the ship? She thought not. If she were a betting woman, she would put her money on him being dead. She didn't know why she wasn't dead. She didn't know how she managed to get away, and a part of her still wasn't convinced that it was true. Maybe this lifeboat was a dream. Perhaps the sound of the water splashing against the sides of the boat was part of that dream. Maybe she was still sitting in the cabin closet beneath the air duct, breathing in the stench of the two that had her trapped. Possibly any minute she was going to wake up and discover she had already turned into one of them.

She was getting even closer now. She could see the dockworkers on Galveston Island milling about, taking care of their duties. Brice said they wouldn't be expecting this ship. It was to dock at the Cruise Terminal on the mainland, deep into trinity bay, with a much larger dock. The radio was broken, and they couldn't possibly have communicated with those on land. She needed to get on land herself and tell everybody what was going on. She needed to prepare them; she needed to warn them.

She was so close now she could make out the words they were saying. She was only about thirty yards out and still paddling furiously. "Help!" She shouted at the top of her lungs.

A skinny older man who was tending ropes took notice of her first. "Aye!" he hollered toward the boat. "Bring it on in here then!"

Ariana paddled even harder, and as the boat neared a smaller dock, the man came to the edge and met her. Ari stood and threw one of the ropes as hard as she could, and the man caught it quickly. He began to pull the lifeboat into the dock, hand over fist.

That was when he got a good look at Ariana. The girl was filthy, and her clothes were stained and torn. Her lips were cracked from a dry mouth. She seemed to be confused, weak, and dizzy. She appeared to be wearing blood-drenched rags, but it was so mangled the man couldn't tell for sure. For all he knew, the girl could be a victim of human trafficking. What was she doing by herself out in the middle of the ocean?

He took Ariana by the hand and helped her to get out of the boat and put her feet firmly on the dock. "What the heck, my dear? You look as if you've been through the wringer."

Ariana was panting hard. She was covered in sweat and blood; she smelled terrible. Ari looked at the man with a stern look on her face. Pointing at the ship out to sea, she said, "See that? They are coming! We have to tell someone. We can't let them dock! Destroy them before they reach land!"

With that, her eyes rolled back in her head, and she fainted.

The dockhand caught her clumsily before she hit the ground. "Aye, I need some aid over here!" A couple of other dock hands rushed toward him.

"What's going on?" one asked as they reached him.

The man shook his head. "I don't know, but she's trying to tell me something about that ship. She said we have to destroy it. She's delusional, I think."

A third man called the medics, and soon they were there. They were securing her on a gurney to put her in the ambulance when she suddenly came to.

"What… What are you doing?" She asked. Her eyes were distant, as if she didn't know where she was.

"We're going to take you to the hospital, miss," said

the first EMT. "You need to be seen. You are dehydrated, your heart is palpitating, and have a major sunburn. You need to calm down mam, or you will go into cardiac arrest."

Ariana sat up straight, her eyes wild. "No! You have to tell them! They're all dead! Don't let them dock!"

One EMT looked at the other, then uncapped a syringe full of sedative. "Here, sweetie," he said, sticking her with the needle and driving the plunger home. "That will make it all better."

Ari's eyes fluttered closed, and her head hit the pillow, no longer worried in the least about the death and destruction that planned to dock in Houston today.

∞

"Sir, we have a cruise ship coming in hot," the port traffic controller voiced with wide eyes. "Judging by its markings, it's the Fantasy Lines Cruise Ship, sir." He said with panic in his voice.

The harbormaster expressed with concern. "That ship is not scheduled for arrival for three more days." He continued, "Have you hailed the Captain?"

"We have tried sir, and we are met with no response. I believe it to be on autopilot, sir. It will try to dock in the scheduled birth."

"I will not have a ship collision on my watch get the other ships out of the way." The harbormaster ordered in a gruff voice. "Get on the horn, call everyone." The port authority was scrambling and trying to make arrangements to move all the other ships. At the same time, David was disembarking the plane at Houston international airport. He was met with a constant busy signal and unable to contact the port.

Surprisingly David's phone rang, breaking his concentration. "David, this is Carl, my search result show a patient by the name of Ariana Harrington was checked into Houston General Hospital. Do you want to check this out, it could be our girl?"

Within moments David was on the phone with the hospital, they were able to identify her with the personalized stateroom key card the cruise lines issued to all guests. Luckily it was in her pocket.

"Keep her secure and quarantine the area. I am en route." David disconnected the call with the hospital.

Without putting the phone down, David made another call. "Ray, I just got off the phone with the doctors treating Ariana. Apparently, she made it to shore, and minutes later passed out. I'm en route to the hospital now. I believe we have a containment issue." David continued to talk to Ray for most of the way to the hospital. Ray was adamant that he was not to mention zombies at all or even use the word for that matter.

∞

"How is she?" David asked the nurse.

"She is stable. You can see her if you like." He followed the nurse into the room.

"Ariana, hello, my name is David Umbridge. I'm from the CDC. I want to commend you for your bravery."

David spent some time with her; she was able to

share her experience. They talked about Captain McElroy and how he was commanding the ship, the flesh-eaters were following his orders. She mentioned the brief conversation she had with her mother. The entire talk shined a new light on David's analogy. These things are smart enough to navigate a ship, if on land, the damage could be insurmountable.

"No one else survived," Ariana said with a tear in her eye. "The ship is completely overrun, it's 'dead on the water,' you need to destroy it."

I'm sorry about your family," David said, overwhelmed with the details she told him.

"I'm going with you, Ariana demanded!" As she drew back the covers and pulled the I.V. from her arm. She stood, searching franticly for her clothes.

David couldn't stop her. She was adamant; he had sympathy for her losing her family to this devastation at hand. What could he do? He was preoccupied with the thought of stopping the ship. Time was running short, and he needed to cut through all the red tape, and fast. David picked up the phone and dialed a childhood friend of his James Domingues. "Hello, Major Domingues, its David," the two reminisced for only a minute till he laid down the facts.

CHAPTER 26

But the truth was that it had only just begun.

The Fantasy Cruise Ship was in plain sight now, and only a couple of hours behind Ariana. There had been no radio call and no forewarning. But now the boat was here.

The dockhand, who people called 'Teddy,' was throwing ropes and clearing the way, yelling this way, and that to others to make the preparations go more smoothly. As the boat neared, its horn blew loudly, almost deafeningly. Teddy looked up at it, and somewhere in the back of his mind, it registered that everyone was standing at the railing looking stoic and grim. His stomach lurched; he had a funny feeling.

The luxury liner was almost settled in its place, emergency crews rushing around when the gate on the main ship opened, and the passengers began to disembark furiously. They waited for no 'okay' or 'all clear.' They just started to file off the ship, with no rhyme or reason. Half of them were staggering around.

Phu-fa-lou weaved her way between the legs of the mass exodus, with what appeared to be a finger clenched tightly between her teeth. A steady stream of drool dripping from below, she was just as eager as the rest of them. Ready to stretch her legs on land.

Teddy kept his eyes fastened on the people as they reached the dock and began to fan out, people going this way and that. They seemed to be groaning loudly, and to be honest, every last one of them looked like they were either dreadfully sick or dead. Something was off.

He saw the captain then, or at least someone wearing the uniform of a captain. He could barely walk a straight line, and he was making his way toward Teddy.

"Sir," Teddy shouted at him. "Are you alright? Your passengers?"

Then he began to hear the screams and the shouts for help. He looked around erratically, trying to see where it was coming from, and just as the captain reached him, Teddy realized it was coming from all around. Everyone was screaming.

"Sir," he began once more as the captain reached him. His arm was outstretched as if he wanted to shake Teddy's hand. Teddy reached for it, but as soon as they took hands, the captain violently pulled the deckhand toward him and sank the few teeth he had left into his neck.

This time, when Teddy heard a scream for help, it was his own.

∞

Apache helicopters swarmed in, and all around the scene, the sound of gunshots rang out in succession.

Troops were everywhere, and the entire port was on lockdown. There was absolutely no way in or out unless you wanted to go for a swim. Bodies were strewn all over the place. The rooftops were covered with sharpshooters under the direct command of the General. Nothing was to come out of the water. "Our position is desperate, but with sheer will, fear, and luck, we will overcome all obstacles." The General stated with optimism in his voice.

In the faraway distance, one could hear the rumble of the artillery. They strafed the fleeing living dead who, had jumped overboard, with machine-gun fire. A stream of lead showering down.

The radio squelched as the General's voice came over. "We have received launch authority; your mission is; complete thermal destruction of the Fantasy Lines Cruise Ship. The entire vessel is to be blanketed, not one square inch missed. Over 3000 civilians and a number of US Marines will lose their lives in this airstrike." The briefing was quick. The threat was imminent.

"Tower this is strike leader, weapon is hot." The pilot announced as he flipped the arming trigger to the air-to-surface Hellfire missiles. "Target acquired rolling in," he continued. "Time on target 12 seconds."

The cruise ship blew with such force. The severity could be heard miles away. Water and chunks of metal fragments showered down upon the harbor, the smell of war reeked. Smoldering rubble was everywhere, as the copters made their second pass, they preceded to drop napalm where the massive luxury liner once stood in all its glory.

David picked up his phone as he exited the expressway. "Hello Major Domingues, its David. I'm at the barricade." David was pulling up to the port; the militaries' show of force was astonishing.

"Excellent, I will inform my men, and have someone escort you to the command post, sit tight." The major let out a sigh and continued. "Umbridge, it was a close call, thank you." He said as he disconnected the line.

David and Ariana were sitting patiently in the rental at the barricade entrance. Within moments they were at the command post observing the destruction that had taken place. The pungent odor of napalm and burnt flesh filled the air. David coughed, as one of the men, handed him a respirator. The entire site looked and smelled like a war zone.

The two stood overlooking the area. As some smoke cleared, Ariana could see one last corpse crawl from the rubble; her eyes grew wide as she focused on the sight before her; it was Adam. She nudged David and pointed in the direction, "that's my brother," she said, but it was too late. Bullets riddled his body from all directions, within moments, nothing was left but chunks of flesh all over the dock. She turned to David as he comforted her while she grieved. Finally, for the first time, Ariana broke down and cried. All the tears that were bottled up inside finally came to ahead.

The poor girl had no one left. He thought to himself

as a tear escaped his eye. The reality was finally hitting David's heart. Right then, he decided he would stay in contact with her. He would check-in on Ariana's wellbeing. The two talked, he mostly listened to her, how could he even imagine what it would be like to lose your entire family in an instant. It was definitely traumatizing. There was no doubt in his mind. He would make sure they exchanged personal contact info, and he would offer a shoulder and ear anytime she needed one. He has no problem being the father figure she so desperately needed after this hellacious event. David was adamant he would certainly be retiring after this massive case, what a way to finish his long career.

The death and destruction on US soil was unsurpassed.

David took a deep breath and picked up his phone once again. He had to make one last call, "Hello Ray, Its David. I'm at the port." David filled Ray in on all the facts. Yes, the situation was grim, but under control.

"Oh, Ray, one last thing. The word Zombie, will be on my report." He said as he disconnected the call.

It was going to be a long night.

∞

The sunset danced on the water, as the sliver of sun disappeared below the horizon. Seagulls and ship horns could be heard in the distance. The water swept over the shore, washing away all the chaos from the day, leaving behind untouched sand. Just then, without warning, a disfigured hand came out of the surf and clawed at the beach.

R.W.K. Clark

CHAPTER 27

Ariana was finally cleared from quarantine and allowed to go home. The realization of the loss of her family finally hitting her in full force. She cried for what seemed like days. She had the massive place all to herself; she was a complete wreck and was all alone.

Ari missed Adam's incessant pestering. She wished he would interrupt her book one last time. Perhaps he could show her one of his videogames? She wanted her mom to invite her shopping. Ariana was sure she could choose something from the store. She needed her dad; they would go on that vacation just the two of them.

The phone rang again. Ariana was ignoring the calls. She just wanted to grieve alone. She missed her family; most of all, she yearned for her dad. There it was again that irritating ring that wouldn't stop. Ari ignored it one last time before heading to bed.

It was late, Ariana was sleeping soundly. She was dreaming of Brice. They were laughing and giggling. He went quiet all of a sudden, she turned to him his eyes were closed, then flew open milky white. Ariana sat up, heart pounding in her chest; it was another nightmare.

The nightmares plagued her sleep.

Ariana's bedroom was quiet, with a weak sound of the curtains blowing in the breeze. It was dark; the air was crisp and refreshing. A faint sound of crickets could be heard in the distance. Ariana rose from her bed and made her way out of her room with her blanket draped around her. She stopped at Adam's door and peered inside for a bit. Then she continued to her father's office, where she sat in his chair, pulling her legs up tight and snuggling in her blanket. The familiar smell of leather and oak comforted her. Within moments she was fast asleep once again.

∞

The phone rang, jolting her from her slumber. The morning sun was peeking through the windows. Ariana rubbed her eyes as she peered at the clock; it was merely daybreak. There it was again that annoying sound. Fed up, she let out an audible sigh and went for the receiver.

"Hello," she said with anger in her tone.

She heard a garbled low animalistic but familiar voice that said, "Sunshine?" That one word sent chills down her spine.

"Daddy?"

Dead on the Water

ENTREATY

This book was made possible by reviews from readers like you. Reviews fuel my creativity. If you enjoyed this novel, I implore you to please write a review and share your experience on the retailer's website. The livelihood for authors is entirely dependent on reviews, and I must say, it is the largest obstacle as a struggling author that I have encountered. Please tell a friend, tell a loved one about this read. With your help, I will be one step closer to overcoming this obstacle. In return, I thank you from the bottom of my heart, and sincerely appreciate your time and effort.

Humbled, with gratitude,

R.W.K. Clark

ABOUT THE AUTHOR

I am a father of two beautiful children, Jon and Kim. They are my motivating forces; they are the lighthouse in this vast ocean. In my life, they are the air that I breathe; they are the oasis in this desert of uncertainty. They are my greatest joy in life and my number one priority. I have a long list of hobbies, and I attribute that to my lust for life! I like to surround myself with positive people, who share the same interests. Family values, the arts, outdoors, nature, and travel are tops on my list. I embrace attending cultural and artistic events because I believe dramatic self-expression is the window to the soul. I wear my heart on my sleeve, and I still believe in chivalry, and I always treat people the way I want to be treated.

www.rwkclark.com

www.ingramcontent.com/pod-product-compliance
Lightning Source LLC
Chambersburg PA
CBHW050021180626
46810CB00002B/517